Gathering Bittersweet

JoHannah Reardon

ISBN-13: 978-1475123050
ISBN-10: 1475123051

DEDICATION

To my sister Jane—may the legend of the rat muff live on!
And to our lovely grandmother, for whom you were named,
who inspired this story in the first place.

1

GATHERING BITTERSWEET

"Rachel, Raacheel…" Fay's call jolted me out of my daydreams as I walked along the shore throwing pebbles into the rushing water. The peace I had been enjoying now shattered at the sound of her panic stricken voice. It had to be Papa. I picked up my skirts, wadding them in a knot by my hip so that I could run faster.

As I approached the house, breathless and frightened, I noticed an unfamiliar horse tied to our fence post. Entering, my eyes first rested on a quiet figure standing in the shadows at the corner of the room. Before my mind could dwell on the question of who it could be, my sister Fay embraced me as she sobbed uncontrollably. I turned my head slowly to look at our father, afraid to see the inevitable.

He laid so quietly, just a wisp of the big man who used to carry me on his shoulders when I was a child. I pulled myself from Fay's grip and walked hesitantly over to his bed. "Oh Papa!" was all I could manage to croak out of my raw throat.

I touched his hand and kissed his forehead, anxious to do these things before he turned cold.

Fay continued to cry, her hands covering her face as she stood helplessly in the center of the room. The figure in the shadows now moved over to Fay. He removed his hat as he nervously turned it around in his large work-worn hands.

"I'm sorry, ma'am. I wish there was somethin' I could've done. Do you want me to fetch the parson?"

Fay pulled herself together through sheer force of will as I had seen her do countless times before. "Yes. Pastor Watson knows that we'd be needing him soon. Thank you ever so much for stopping."

With that, the strange man dropped his hat onto his head and rushed out of the house with a relieved look on his face.

Fay and I were alone, feeling like two baby birds whose mother was just shot out of the air. I knew Fay's tears were not for grief alone but fear for our future. We seemed to have nothing to say to one another at this awful moment.

Fay sank into a chair, leaning her head on her crossed arms. I went back outside to my beloved river but the rapid movement of the water, which had comforted me a moment before, now sounded harsh and demanding as if it were washing my life away with the current. My tears joined the flow of water surrounding me, making me feel as I did when it rained for days on end, listless and without a desire for anything. At the dawn of each day for seventeen years I'd risen to my father's voice. Now I'd never hear it again.

I pulled my knees up to my chest, wrapping my arms around them and rocked myself back and forth as a mother rocks a child. My body ached for someone larger and stronger to hold me and comfort me, but there was no one so my own two arms were all I could use to ease my pain. I don't know how long I remained in this position, except when I unwound myself I was so stiff that I could hardly move. When I finally stood, I thought of Fay. Guilt pushed me back to the house, although I felt that I never wanted to enter it again. All I really wanted to do was to put our small boat on the water and let the river take me where it would, but that would never do. I'd have to come back some day so I might as well face it now.

When I stepped into the darkness of our kitchen, I was shocked to see Fay busy preparing dinner. "We might as well eat early. I've got to go into town and wire Emily. We are going to join her and Adam in Montana. I've given the entire matter a lot of thought. We can't stay here alone, Rachel." Fay had that determined look which defied any disagreement.

I nodded my head and began setting the table, amazed that she could cook dinner with our father growing cold in the next room. And I knew better than to argue with her. Even if I objected to joining our sister and her husband, it would matter little. Twelve years my senior, Fay raised me since our mother died when I was a baby. She made the decisions, even when Papa was alive.

"Who was that man, Fay?"

"Just a passer-by. Father saw him out the window and told me to call him in. By the time I returned he'd quit breathing." Fay's voice trailed off into a whisper as she fought her emotions. The quiver in her voice caused my throat to constrict and made further conversation impossible.

Somehow we got through that awful dinner. Without speaking, Fay shoveled the food into her mouth, while I mostly stirred mine around the plate. Each time I got close to my mouth with a bite, my stomach flipped like a fish out of water. Fortunately, Fay was too caught up in her own emotions to notice. I moved things around enough that it looked like I'd eaten a bit.

The parson arrived as soon as we finished dinner. His face looked as sober as if it had been his own father who had passed on. He stared at the ground most of the time and shook his head side to side repeatedly. Quoting Scripture and murmuring condolences, his voice became a hum in my ears like a mosquito's buzz. Relief flooded over me as he and Fay solemnly made their way into the other room to make the funeral arrangements while I washed the dishes. As the water swished in the dishpan, my tears began again in earnest, turning the dishtowel into a giant handkerchief.

The day of the funeral was even worse. Folks from all over came to help us commit Papa to the dust. Some of them I hadn't seen in years, but the whole countryside turns out for a funeral. I hated repeating the same meaningless nonsense over and over to each person as they tried to "comfort me in my sorrow." None of them were very good at it, so I began to feel that I was in a dream state I couldn't shake. My emotions went numb that day. I quit crying and nodded to each person as they continued to mutter sayings they'd heard others impart during funerals of their own. You'd think with all that practice someone would figure out something useful to say like, "This is horrible, isn't it? I hate it" or "I can't think of anything to say at a time like this because there just isn't anything to say." Not that these words would really do anything except make me feel like people were being honest. The only good thing about the funeral was that by the end of it the numbness had passed and I was so mad I could have kicked a mule. Mad felt better than sad, so I stayed there a while.

Not that anyone noticed. Fay continued on with our plans without consulting my feelings whatsoever. She noticed my banging things around a little more than usual. I know, because she said, "Stop that right now, Rachel. You're giving me a headache." So that was that. I had to be mad by myself.

She decided we'd go see our mother's brother, Uncle Charles, before settling in Montana. He lived in Illinois, two days of train travel from our home in Bevel, Missouri.

We'd only been to see him once before in our lives, and I'd been pretty young then. I could recall him being a dignified, quiet man. The trip didn't sound very exciting. But then again, nothing sounded very exciting. I just couldn't find enthusiasm for anything. If I could, I would have given Fay a piece of my mind about what I wanted to do, but I had no idea what I wanted to do, so I let her lead me like a little lost lamb.

The day we left for the train station with all our worldly possessions in our trunks, I looked back at the only house I'd known. The new tenants arrived just as we were leaving. As they waved cheerfully at our passing buggy, my anger flared again. How dare they be so happy about our shattered lives! I knew that wasn't fair, but I chose to feel that way anyway.

I'll say this for the parson—he practiced what he preached. His buggy was the one taking us to the station. He unloaded our trunks himself and hugged us both as though we were long lost daughters, even though we barely knew him. He'd just recently moved to the area and we were not regular churchgoers. I've got to admit that I felt warmly toward him at that moment.

We boarded the train without a backward glance as the steam rushed from the engine, so loud I could barely hear the people talking next to me. As we pulled out of the station, I watched the town, which I knew better than my own face, recede in the distance. As the sound of the train bumping over the rails filled my mind, I tried to shake off the numbness of the last few weeks. I hadn't yet learned that sorrow can make us wise if we let it do its work, therefore I found myself in a prison of my own making, seeing only that life as I had known it was gone forever.

My mind wandered back to my father. In all my seventeen years, it was he who brought the joy into our daily tasks. Fay kept the order and the discipline, and Papa gave us laughter. I loved to sit by his side after a hard day of work and listen to his stories. My favorite was his account of when, as a little boy, he saw Abraham Lincoln pass in a carriage while he was visiting St. Louis. It brought a smile to my face now and broke my dismal mood as I thought of my father as a child, enchanted at seeing the president.

As I gazed out the window, watching the fields pass in a blur, I tossed around questions like a flock of birds circling a field. Would I ever see him again? I wanted to think that Papa had gone to a better place but I had no basis for this assurance. I wanted to believe in God, yet mine was a vague belief. Inside I balled my fist and muttered, "Why, God, did you take him?" When someone dies, whom can we blame but God? Yet even as I blamed him, I felt that I was shaking my fist in ignorance.

"Why do you do this to yourself?" I muttered under my breath. I'm not a moody personality so it always disgusts me when my disposition is overtaken by emotion, which had been pretty much a constant state for the last few weeks. I forced myself to think of something else. Maybe it would do me good to move about. I slipped out of my seat and walked up the aisle. It always made me feel like giggling when I tried to walk in a moving train. I was sure this must be how a toddler feels when he is taking his first steps.

I almost made it the length of the train when the railcar I was in careened sharply to the left. The motion threw me on top of a young man seated near me. I began to gather myself to rise; I knew by the burning on my cheeks that they had turned scarlet. I was sure of it when I looked this man in the face. His initial reaction had been one of surprise, but his expression changed as his smile spread across his face like a sunrise peeking over the horizon.

"Well, an angel from heaven has plopped upon my lap," he laughed. He was a handsome man with very blond hair; it had not browned as so many blondes do. His eyes were a cool, clear blue, and he had a fine chiseled nose. I could tell by his suit that he was a man of means, young though he be. He wore an air of complete confidence, as though he controlled all circumstances.

"I'm sorry—the train—I didn't mean to!" I stammered in humiliation. I now became aware of the other passengers looking at me in disapproval, although I detected a glimmer of amusement on an elderly man's face.

"Now, I don't think it's a bit awful. It made a dull ride a lot more interesting." I was at once both attracted to and repulsed by this gentleman, if a gentleman indeed he was.

I had an overriding feeling that I should get back to Fay as quickly as possible. This was not the kind of man with whom one felt safe.

"I'm glad to have amused you for a moment, but I must get back to my sister," I responded acidly, more to assuage my wounded pride than out of contempt for this man.

"Now wait a minute," he reached for my hand as he spoke. "I don't even know your name."

"Rachel, Rachel Scott. I must go now," I answered more civilly this time, although I pulled my hand back as if a snake had bit it.

Trying to hurry down that rocking railcar was almost impossible, fearing each moment that I'd land on someone else's lap. What worried me more was that I felt his eyes following me all the way, sending quivers of fear up and down my spine. Whether this was a good or bad feeling, I wasn't sure.

When I reached Fay again, the humor of the situation struck me. I giggled to myself as I thought of the foolish picture I made and the look of shock on the young man's face. I decided not to tell Fay about the episode. It would only upset her. Later she would think it was funny, but now she would be concerned for my dignity and the propriety of it all. Yes, it would be a secret between that young man and me. I tucked my hair back into its tidy bun and smoothed my wrinkled skirts. I was already a mess.

What a sight I would be after a day and a night in a train. That thought made me giggle again. Fay had been resting, but now she opened one eye to peer at me. I quickly sobered up on the outside but continued to chuckle within. Perhaps my trek through the railcars had helped my gloomy mood after all.

My thoughts began to slowly trickle in another direction, as the beginning of a waterfall wears a new path in the stone. Maybe change isn't so bad after all. Who knows what could be in store for me now? If Papa were alive, I would most certainly have spent my entire life in Missouri. Even if the circumstances for leaving were depressing, I was offered a new chance at life. In the astounding resilience of the young, the adventure of the unknown began to replace the loss of the familiar. To my amazement, it was not just relief but anticipation that gripped me when the conductor announced our stop in Wesley, Illinois.

2

SPRING IN WESLEY

As we stepped out of the train into the beautiful sunshine, I was gripped by the feeling of hope that was slowly growing within me. Still, I was almost dizzy from so much time on the train and from the weight of my thoughts. Somehow the move into the bright light exaggerated these things. I was rather relieved that Uncle Charles was not yet at the station. It gave me a chance to get my bearings.

It had been a long time since I'd been to Illinois. I'd forgotten how open central Illinois is. One could look for miles without any obstruction. Just seeing all that space caused my soul to expand within me. The spring was just beginning. I could see a mass of spring beauties pushing their way through the earth in front of a nearby home. It looked as though Illinois had as severe a winter as Missouri by the way the paint was peeling on the little house with the flowers. Looking the other way into the country, the horizon went on forever. The black dirt of freshly overturned fields contrasted with the prairie grass blowing in the gentle breeze. Illinois is not the kind of place with which one falls immediately in love, but it grows on you just as its fertile soil causes other living things to grow.

"Rachel, you look awfully pale." I was startled when Fay spoke to me. She had been so silent on this journey. It was in character that her first words in a while were uttered out of concern for me. I wondered what her thoughts might have been on our long trek.

"I'm fine Fay, just tired from the journey. Do you think Uncle Charles has forgotten that we are coming today?"

"No, I'm sure he hasn't. However, he probably is busy in the fields. It may be hard for him to get away. Please don't say anything to make him feel bad about being late." Fay was always warning me about things that I had no intention of doing. Possibly she had observed me sticking my foot in my mouth a few too many times.

"Would you like something to eat, Rachel? I have some buttered bread left from the food I brought."

"You eat it, Fay. I couldn't eat a thing." I often wished my appetite were as good as Fay's. She always ate well and had a beautiful curvy figure. Food rarely appealed to me even though I knew that I was painfully thin. I wished I could eat now just to help wile away the time.

Instead of eating, I decided to observe my new surroundings. Only one other person had gotten off at this station. She was a middle-aged woman who was greeted by a tall, slender gentleman with a neatly trimmed beard and a well-dressed woman who was rather portly but had a twinkle in her eyes when she smiled. There was something about her eyes that struck me. They were hazel colored with flecks of green, but that wasn't what caught my attention. It was how her eyes lit up her face when she smiled. It melted all my reserve and made me feel like hugging her, certainly a reaction I'd never had toward a stranger before. I stared at her until I felt self-conscious, unable to tear my gaze away. I liked the couple immediately by the loving way they welcomed the woman at the station. I hoped that these friendly people were typical of those in this small town, and I particularly wanted to get to know these two. Even as she walked out of the station, I tried to get a glimpse of her amazing eyes.

As soon as they left the station, the ordinariness of the place crushed down upon me. It was small, but clean. The ticket master came out from behind his desk and swept the floor of the fresh spring mud that many shoes deposited. Working in a train station would not be a bad job. A person would see much of the good and bad in life and as long as one could meet many different kinds of people, it shouldn't become too boring. I had begun to think a lot about how Fay and I would make a living. There were so few things that women could do. I felt great sympathy toward the suffragettes. If women were able to vote, who knows what else might open up to them? I was thankful that Fay had taught me to sew and embroider early in life since I had no mother to teach me. It was a way to make something beautiful, which I always longed to do, and also helped with the needs of our small family.

"Fay, do you think that I'll be able to earn money as a seamstress in Montana?"

"I thought of that, Rachel. It may be just what you need to do. I think that the towns out there would need women skilled in such necessary things, and you are a wonderful seamstress. I'd trust your stitches in a cyclone. Emily seems to think that we will be able to make our way there, so that's enough for me. Of course, Adam wants to take care of us any way he can."

I looked back at the ticket master and thought how his job would never appeal to Fay. She couldn't stand idle time. I filled time with my hands and my thoughts, but she needed to be active, which made her excellent at running a household. I think she could run a business as well. When we'd discussed going to Montana, I'd suggested that she open a restaurant. Her cooking was superb and I wanted to decorate the place. She brushed my idea aside with a "wait and see" attitude.

"Maybe we should try to find…" Fay began, when a man we'd never met approached.

"You be Fay and Rachel Scott?"

"Yes, we are."

"Welcum to Wesley! I'm John, Charles Bradbury's hir'd man. He sends his 'poligies. He's just fixin' ta cum meet ya when a neighbor ova the way cum 'fo his help. He din't even take time to 'splain ta me what the problim was but sent me ta git ya. I think he spens too much time helpin' otha foks, hasn't time ta do his own work, but he don' listen ta me none."

"Well, thank you for coming, John." Fay's response was all politeness, but her forehead wrinkled and she got that look of disapproval on her face that always made me fear what was next.

"These all your stuff? I can tell yer fine ladies with so many bags and trunks."

"This is all we own in the world, John. We have no permanent home right now, so we must bring all of this with us."

"Yes'm. I's mighty sorry ta hear 'bout your Pa. Mista Bradbury thought he ta be a fine man. He's shore glad ya 'cided ta cum see him."

As John loaded our things into the buckboard, it gave me a chance to take stock of him. Although a rather short man, he seemed large due to his squarely built physique. The way he heaved our heavy trunks into the wagon showed that he was no stranger to physical labor. Dressed in overalls and a flannel shirt, it was his hat that stood out. Made of knitted wool in at least five different colors, it fit tightly on his head. I'd never seen one like it but thought it looked practical. He had a brisk but cheerful manner and I decided I liked him.

I thought again of Fay's troubled look as John told her why Uncle Charles couldn't meet us. Whether she was concerned for the neighbor, Uncle Charles, or us, I couldn't tell. I don't think it was out of contempt for John. At least if that was her initial reaction, she'd softened toward him now.

"Neva' been to Missoura. What's it like?"

"Near Kansas City, where we're from, it's fairly wooded and wet. Bevel is close to the Missouri River. There's a lot of farm land around there but our soil isn't nearly this black and rich." I could tell this last comment pleased him. Fay was talking his language.

"Nothin' like Illinois black dirt. I hear no state save Ioway come close ta havin' soil like ours. Yer Pa farm, did 'e?"

"Yes, he did. He worked too hard, I'm afraid," Fay had always worried about him overdoing it. Sadly her warnings finally came true.

"They ain't nothin' like farmin'. It be hard work awright, but the rewards're so great. Afta knockin' yourself out all spring, seein' them corn sta'ks poke through the ground gives a real thrill. Kinda like raisin' a baby, I s'pose, though I don' know much 'bout that."

"Have you always lived in Illinois, John?" I finally entered the conversation out of curiosity about his accent.

"Nope. I cum from Ohio a few years back, but was raised in Virginy. That's why I can really 'preciate this place. I've seen how stubburn farm land can be. I's lucky, too, ta be workin' fo a man like yer uncle. Couldn't ask fo a fairer man ta work fo."

We rode in silence for a few moments and then John began once more. "Speakin' of Illinois dirt, thar's a great story 'bout a man who cum here frum the East. He'd toiled his farm for years tryin' ta raise corn, and comin' through Illinois ta go West, he stopped fur the night and whilst grindin' corn fo his dinner, he dropped a few kernels in the soil. By mornin' they sprouted and he stayed right thar. They say he's got the biggest farm in Illinois now." He turned to us and winked which brought a smile to both of us.

John chatted with us all the way to Uncle Charles' farm. Somehow being out of the musty, noisy train and riding again in the open air lifted my spirits like an eagle soaring off the cliffs. It truly was a beautiful spring day. My dizziness disappeared and I began to feel the freshness and hope that spring brings to all of us.

3

MEADOW BROOK STOCK FARM

As we pulled up to Uncle Charles' farm, John had me giggling and even managed to get Fay to chuckle. Neither of us had felt this good in weeks. When Fay looked into my eyes, we both knew that coming to Illinois had been a good decision.

The farm looked just as I'd remembered it. Uncle Charles had been successful like many Illinois farmers. The land here was rich and yielded well to hard work. Uncle Charles, however, was not one for show. His home was of modest size. He'd never married so did not feel a need for a large place.

Clearly, he took great pride in the farm. The house was whitewashed perfectly and shaded by a large sugar maple in the front. The leaves were still the light green of early spring, but I knew they would be a brilliant gold in the fall. I wistfully wished we would be here to see it, but knew we'd be far away from here by then. It was the weeping willow in the back, though, of which I had such great memories. I remember Uncle Charles sitting there with me years ago. He and Papa loved to swap stories and sing under its tent-like branches. A lover of trees, he also had a clump of white birch and a sprawling redbud tree in his yard. A path in the back yard, lined with crocuses, led to a vegetable garden. To the left of the garden stood a grape arbor, my favorite spot in August. During our last visit, I was small enough that I had to reach up to the vines as I stuffed myself so full of grapes that I couldn't eat my dinner. Uncle Charles defended my right to do so when my father scolded me.

To the right of the house were his bright red barns. They contrasted brilliantly with the green meadow and cool brook, which surrounded them, giving the farm its name: Meadow Brook Stock Farm. The hired hand's place was near these barns, and gleamed as freshly painted and clean as Uncle Charles' own house.

Evidently our uncle had not yet returned from the neighbors, so John helped us to our room. We shared a large room that had three windows, two of them with a western exposure, making it very bright at this time of day. What made the room seem even bigger was that it had so few furnishings in it. Besides an oak bed and chest of drawers, the only thing in the room was a small table with a vase of fresh flowers on it, and a dry sink for washing.

Fay and I immediately used the sink for we both felt grimy as a pig that's been wallowing in the mud. We changed clothes and sponged out all the stains in our travel garments, laying them over the bed to dry. After this we

JoHannah Reardon

unpacked our bags and lay down to rest. We must have both fallen asleep for a long while because when I awoke, the room was no longer bright and shadows were beginning to change the whole mood of the place.

"Fay, wake up," I whispered. "I think it's late. Uncle Charles probably is beginning to wonder if we ever plan to greet him."

"Oh! I had no idea we'd slept so long. Let's do hurry."

We straightened our hair and dresses and then hurried down the stairs. A couple of steps ahead of Fay, I first heard a commotion in the kitchen. Sure enough, there was Uncle Charles, hardly changed at all from the last time I saw him. Tall and slender, he sported a beard that was just starting to turn the slightest bit of gray. When he saw me, he dropped the pan in his hand and rushed over to embrace me and then Fay, his arms around both of us at once.

"Rachel, Fay, it's so wonderful to have you here. I'm glad you got some rest after that long train ride. You woke up just in time for supper."

"I'll get our aprons so we can help you, Uncle Charles."

"Too late, Fay. Everything's ready. I was just cleaning up the mess I'd made."

We sat down right in the kitchen to eat. Even though Uncle Charles had a dining room, he rarely used it. He'd prepared a simple but delicious meal of roast carrots, potatoes, and beef, which smelled good even to me. Neither Fay nor I were shy about eating this first night in Illinois. "There's plenty where that came from. Don't they have any food left in Missouri?" he asked with a grin.

What impressed me more than the meal was the prayer that Uncle Charles said before we ate. We said grace before our meals at home, at least on Sundays, but it was a memorized prayer. Uncles Charles spoke to God as if he knew Him personally. I even opened my eyes during the prayer to see if there was anything supernatural that had materialized in the room as he spoke. I decided to question him about this later.

"Girls, I want to express my great sorrow at your father's passing. He was like a brother to me. In fact, since I'm considerably younger than your mother, I knew him almost as long as I knew her. There was never a time that I did not enjoy being with him. He had a way of making the world a merrier place."

I felt a lump in my throat as he said these things but the more he spoke, the easier it became to chase away those feelings.

"We both shared a love for music. Your father spoke often of the Swedish singer, Jenny Lind, whom he heard and never forgot her lovely voice. I believe your middle name came from her, didn't it Rachel?" I nodded and he continued. "I have always felt I had a heritage in music

because my great-uncle was the famous hymn writer
William B. Bradbury. Perhaps after dinner, I could play
some of his hymns on the piano and we could sing
together. Remember doing that when you were here
years ago with your father?"

"Indeed I do, Uncle Charles. It's one of my best memories,
you and Papa singing together…." My mind skipped over
the past in dreamy remembrance, the way a flat stone
skips over water when it's thrown.

"Well, we can make all new memories now, starting
tonight. I'll call John in too. He does a marvelous job
playing the fiddle. He can turn a hymn into a foot-
stomping event. Are you sure you girls are up to all this
tonight?"

Our only answer was a delighted giggle.

We cleared the dishes and washed them in record time
that evening. John did indeed come with his fiddle and we
sang until our voices sounded croaky like the frogs that
were kicking up a fuss outside. The evening ended with all
of us sitting by the fire listening to John's tall tales. I soon
learned not to believe everything he said, but I still
enjoyed his ability to stretch the truth into an adventure.

When the hour grew late and John left for his own home,
Fay and I sat chatting with Uncle Charles until the wee
hours of the night. What a wonderful thing family is. It
was so fine to converse with someone who knew my
parents well. Daniel and Abigail were young again as

Uncle Charles spoke of their courtship and their journey to Missouri. Being my mother's younger brother, he'd been full of pranks, such as the time he took a bite out of every item of a carefully arranged fruit bowl that she'd prepared for my father. Many of my own childish jokes came back to me as he relayed his stories. As he spoke, I began to see myself as a link in time that passes as quickly as the dandelions that dotted the landscape. I felt an urgency to live my life to the fullest. Surely to do that, I would need to be married. How important that seemed to me as I sat reflecting on the brevity of life. In a moment of silence, I impulsively asked, "Why did you never marry, Uncle Charles?"

He smiled broadly in response to my question, although Fay threw me a troubled look. "Everyone has been trying to get me married for the last twenty years. It's a rather complicated question you ask. I could answer it simply by saying that the right woman never came along, but that is not entirely true." He paused for a moment staring into the fire.

"About fifteen years ago, there was a special girl. Her name was Jill. She was the sweetest person I've ever known. What made her sweet was her love for God. All she wanted out of life was to serve Him." Uncle Charles' voice cracked like a boy of fourteen but he quickly shook it off and went on. "I couldn't see this devotion she had to her Maker," he added in a haughty voice, "so in order to help her get her feet on the ground, as I saw it, I refused to attend church at all. She was heartbroken because she

23

cared for me, but I held my ground." His shoulders now slumped and he spoke in a softer voice. "A short time later Jill died in a train accident."

"Oh, Uncle Charles, I never knew…" Fay began. I remained silent, fighting within as I felt Uncle Charles' loss on top of my own.

"Don't feel sorry for me," Uncle Charles countered, shaking his head. "Jill gave me the greatest gift one can give another. In my brokenness, I turned to her Master, trusted Him with my life. I found that all that mattered was the one thing she had found. In answer to your question, Rachel, I've never felt a need to marry since then. God has given me many rich relationships and much to do for Him."

Neither Fay nor I commented again. It seemed time to end the evening on this sober note. We collapsed into our bed, thoughtful but content. Music and laughter had come back into my life. Both have such a healing effect. And Uncle Charles' melancholy story stirred something inside the way a cook stirs a stew that has been simmering a while. We'd been so busy all evening that I'd forgotten to ask Uncle Charles what the neighbor's trouble had been. I'd be sure to ask him in the morning.

4

THE NEIGHBORS

Fay and I rose early on the morrow to prepare Uncle Charles' breakfast. Fay planned a wonderful meal of bacon, eggs, cornbread, and preserves to surprise him when he came in from the morning chores. It was clear from his look of delight that this was a pleasant change from having to fix his own breakfast after already working hard in the morning.

John joined us, too. "'Ate ta hurt yo feelin's, Mista Bradbury, but this looks a mite betta than you fix."

"Now John, be careful. You're going to have to eat my cooking again someday," Uncle Charles said with a twinkle in his eye. "But I must admit you girls have outdone yourselves."

As everyone hungrily shoveled food in their mouths, I asked Uncle Charles about the neighbor. "Was it something serious that you had to tend to yesterday for the neighbor, Uncle Charles?" I noticed Fay's eyes flashing at me. She clearly thought I should not be asking about the situation unless Uncle Charles first volunteered the information. However, his answer relaxed her disapproval and even provoked her curiosity.

"I'm glad you asked, Rachel. Rather than explain it, I'll take you over there after my fieldwork is done for the day. You might as well meet the Sowders family if you are going to be here for a while."

"Aw, Mista Bradbury, you ought'n take this fine lady ova there. She's too good ta meet the likes of them Sowders."

"Now John, we may be in just as much need as they are someday. Who knows how we might have turned out if we'd the hardship they've seen."

"Hardship, bah! They's just lazy good-fo-nothins. Neva did do an honest day's work."

"Be that as it may, they are our neighbors and it is the second command to 'love our neighbor'. It won't hurt Rachel a bit to learn to obey Jesus' commands better, now will it?"

John answered with only a grunt but it was clear that Uncle Charles had won this argument. As for me, I was quite curious but a little scared to meet the Sowders. I wasn't sure I'd be as good at keeping Jesus' second command as Uncle Charles. I knew I didn't keep the first command of "loving God with all my heart, soul, mind and strength" as well as he did and I felt the second somehow depended on the first.

Sensing the uneasiness at the table, Uncle Charles changed the subject. "Exactly how long do you girls plan to delight us with your company?"

"Just until summer is over, Uncle Charles. We'll head for Montana in the early fall so that we can get settled there before the winter sets in," replied Fay.

"Well, you know that you are welcome to stay the winter here, too, if you like. It has brightened the household considerably to have you here. If you keep cooking like this though, I'll get fat."

That got a laugh out of all of us. I knew by looking at him that I took after my mother's side of the family in build. It would take a great many huge breakfasts to get him to look the least bit fat.

With breakfast over and John and Uncle Charles back to work, Fay began to think about dinner. She could always do that but I never even tried to help her. When I'm full, I cannot even think of food in any way.

So as she planned, I went through Uncle Charles' work clothes, mending and patching anything that looked the least bit worn. After that I took out a table runner that I'd been embroidering during the train trip. I decided that this was just the kind of thing Uncle Charles needed to brighten his tidy little home. He had very few decorative things, which I attributed to his being a bachelor rather than a dislike for such items.

As I stitched, I began to think again about the kind of man Uncle Charles was. I certainly had never known anyone quite like him. It frightened me a little because I knew that to be like him would require a great deal from a person. One part of me desperately wanted to live as he did; another part of me fled from the thought. It seemed best to observe and learn from him but not to let such thinking affect me completely as it had him. Little did I know that when one begins to think differently, one begins to live differently too. I never was very good figuring out cause and effect.

As the day wore on, I began to become anxious for Uncle Charles to take me to meet the Sowders. Not because I wanted to see them so badly, but more because I wanted to see how Uncle Charles reacted to them.

Afternoon shadows finally cast their long silhouettes over the land and Uncle Charles came in to wash up and prepare for our visit. He asked Fay to pack one of the pies she'd made to take to the Sowders family. She was glad to do so for she always loved to share her cooking, but she did not want to accompany us on the visit itself.

We set out with the buckboard because the Sowders lived a couple of miles away. As we were going, I decided now might be a good time to ask some of my questions.

"Uncle Charles, I know you believe in God. I do too, but I'm awfully confused right now. I've always been taught that God is loving. If that's so, why did He take my father away from us, leaving us with no one?" As soon as these words left my mouth, I felt silly and childish for saying them, like a spoiled girl who was always given too much candy, but Uncle Charles treated my question very seriously.

"You were taught correctly, Rachel. God is loving. In fact, He loves us more than we can imagine. It's easy to believe that when all goes well with us. I've had the same struggle that you are going through many times, but I've learned to look at it like this. When your father was alive, did he ever correct you or instruct you? Did he ever point you into a different direction when he thought you needed it?"

"Of course."

"Well, God is the perfect father. He's always disciplining us for our good. That doesn't necessarily mean that we are doing something bad and are being punished. It may mean that He wants us to look squarely into His face so that He can guide us in the best way."

"How can we look God in the face?"

"By turning away from our own desires and seeking His. You will find that the more you do that, the more your desires will become His own."

"But I don't know how to do that."

"Perhaps you need time to get to know Him. That's why He's given us the Bible. Read the gospel of John in your New Testament, Rachel. You'll know Him much better by the time you finish."

We arrived at the Sowders' all too soon. I had a million more questions, but a light began to break through the gloom inside me the way the sun peaks around the curtains in the early hours of the morning.

If the light was beginning to glow, it was all but extinguished when I saw the Sowders' place. Most of the paint had completely peeled off the wood of the small house. There was very little green grass in the yard, if you could call it a yard, as it was mostly mud after all the spring rains. No one had ever bothered to plant trees or flowers, which gave the place a desolate feeling.

I held my skirts high as we walked across a plank someone had thrown over the mud in front of the steps. Uncle Charles helped me up the steps so that I wouldn't fall through the many missing boards. As he knocked on the door, I heard the sound of several children crying. After knocking patiently and persistently, the door finally opened. A girl, not much older than I, stood in a soiled dress. It looked as though she had tried to put her hair up in the morning but most of it was hanging down in dirty strings now. She had a baby crying on one hip and a toddler hanging onto her dress rubbing his muddy face. Behind her I could see three more children. The oldest couldn't have been more than five years old.

When she saw that it was Uncle Charles at the door, she broke into a shy grin and opened the door a little farther. Beyond her I saw that the entire house consisted of one room. There was a fireplace on the east wall with a rocking chair close to it. A large table with backless benches and dirty dishes all over it stood a little way into the room. Opposite of these were the beds, two large ones, a cradle and a small cot. I noticed that the quilts on the beds looked like they'd been washed a thousand times and left in the sun to dry until their colors had washed together. I wondered if that was from the hard use five children gave them or if she'd started married life without new ones. Most striking about the inside of the house was how dark it was. There were only two small windows, both of which were dirty, so that they let through little light, looking more like a way to collect mud than to see out of. Even at this late hour of the day, no lamps were burning.

"Hello, Helen. I came to see how little Howard was doing today. His high fever gave me an awful scare yesterday. I'm sure glad I could get Doc Jamison over to see him."

"Thank ye Mr. Bradbury. He's a mite better today but still real weak. It's the cough that worries me the most now. Don't hardly stop for a minute."

I then noticed the little boy coughing uncontrollably. He took a breath between hacks and smiled weakly when Uncle Charles picked him up.

"It's all right, little Howard. That medicine Doc gave you is helping already, and he'll be back tomorrow to check you again." At this Howard let his little body go limp as he rested on Uncle Charles' shoulder. He seemed more content now, coughing only occasionally.

"Helen, this is my niece, Rachel Scott. She'll be staying with me for the summer along with her sister, Fay. Fay sent you one of her wonderful pies, which will be sure to pick up your spirits."

"Pleased to meet ye, ma'am," said Helen with a nod of her head, but she didn't look pleased at all, only embarrassed.

Because of this, I felt an urgency to make her more comfortable with my presence. "Thank you, Helen. I'm glad Uncle Charles brought me to meet you. I don't know anybody here yet. May I hold the baby?" I said this only to be polite but when I took her in my arms, she immediately quit crying. I've never been that good with infants, so I was surprised.

"What's her name?"

"Lizabeth; we call her Beth."

"I've always loved the name, Beth!" By this time I was completely taken in by this little bundle, dirty face and all.

Helen and Uncle Charles continued talking for a while until Howard fell asleep on his shoulder. He then laid him on the bed, which he shared with two of his brothers, and we began our journey home.

"Thanks, Uncle Charles. I understand why you wanted to take me now." He said nothing in return, and we made the rest of the trip in silence.

I didn't fall asleep so easily this night. I had much to think about. Poor Fay tried to adjust herself in bed as I tossed and turned. My mind kept floating around to different subjects as clouds circle the sky on a windy day. Why do some people have it so difficult in life? Why don't they try harder? Why should we who do try put up with them? Is there anything we can do to make it better for their children? What does God have to say about the poor? Is it His problem or ours? Would looking into God's face, as Uncle Charles put it, help the Sowders family? Would it help me to put up with them?

Eventually the clouds quit moving and settled into a fog in my brain. When sleep finally came, it was peaceful.

5

DISCOVERY

I awoke with a start. For the first time since Papa's death, my waking thoughts were of something other than him. Fay still slept and the sun had not yet peeked over the horizon. However, the birds were singing, the turtledove cooing, and the rooster breaking the silence with his crows, so I knew that dawn was close at hand.

In spite of my effort to be quiet as I washed and dressed, Fay soon stirred. Sleepily, she rubbed her eyes, reminding me of the young Beth in my arms yesterday. Her voice cracked as she used it for the first time that day. "You've been awfully quiet since you went with Uncle Charles yesterday. What happened?"

"Oh Fay, this family was like nothing I've ever seen before. I thought we were poor until I saw the way they live. Helen Sowders can't be much older than I am but she has five children. Can you imagine?" I spoke rapidly, too rapidly for an early morning discussion. Fay clearly thought I'd involved myself more than I should have.

"I think maybe John was right. It doesn't sound like a suitable place to take you," Fay said with a pout on her face. I decided to slow down and speak more carefully.

"I must admit I was feeling the same way when we arrived, but I have quite another attitude now." I paused for some thought and a deep breath, then proceeded with the ideas that had just been forming in my mind. "How can we ever learn any of the answers to life unless we are exposed to life as it is?" As I said these words, I felt some guilt because I knew this was all a theory that I had not tested.

Before Fay could say anything, I changed the topic of our discussion because I wanted Fay's opinion on more than the Sowders. "Uncle Charles and I had a thought-provoking talk about God. I want to believe as he does."

Fay now looked surprised. "I don't know, Rachel. You've always believed in God. We were raised that way even if we haven't been to church in a while."

"But Fay, our faith has no answers. It provides no purpose or meaning for the things we do."

"Things have purpose in themselves, Rachel. You're looking too intensely at the whole matter."

"Maybe you're right." I sighed and rubbed my forehead as the thoughts again began circling like vultures. "I just wish I were more certain about it." I looked up at Fay with a smile, willing the scavengers of my mind away. "By the way, Helen was very pleased with the pie you sent." I could tell this gratified Fay. She has a kind heart.

After breakfast and chores, I decided to go sit under the beloved willow tree and read the gospel of John as Uncle Charles had suggested. Since our discussion, I'd felt a growing hunger to find out for myself if I could know God as Uncle Charles did. Before I began reading, however, I lay down and looked up into the tree. I'd often climbed this tree when I was younger. Its curling soft branches and delicate leaves had provided an enchanting shelter. I remember staying up there until my legs cramped.

A perfect seventy degrees, the weather made me want to stay out here for hours. I pulled my sweater around my shoulders as I breathed the fresh air into my heart. The sound of a cardinal calling at the uppermost part of the tree, the lowing of the cattle in the distance and the soft fur of a kitten as it rubbed against my legs filled me with wonder. It was one of those perfect moments you wish you could freeze for the future when things are stormy and dark.

Somehow this reflection helped the state of my mind as I opened my Bible. My soul was already full of God's handiwork, which made my heart more ready to hear His whisper. I planned to read a couple of chapters a day. I learned many Bible stories as a child and memorized verses in school, but I'd not read the Bible myself at any time. It seemed odd to me now that a book that had so influenced my life, I'd never even read.

"In the beginning was the Word, and the Word was with God, and the Word was God. The same was in the beginning with God. All things were made by him; and without him was not any thing made that was made. In him was life; and the life was the light of men." So began my reading in the first chapter of John. I don't know how much time went by, but I finished all twenty one chapters in the book. I couldn't put it down. The Jesus in this book was so different from the sad pictures of him displayed at church. The circumstances of His birth, which I'd heard a thousand times before, took on new meaning, as I understood who He was. He was with God in the beginning. I marveled at the thought of Jesus leaving a throne of glory to be born a humble babe in a manger.

In the first five chapters, I wondered at His teaching just as those who encountered him then did. Yet, it was in chapter five that Jesus proclaimed that He was equal with God. Here was more than a good teacher. Here was one who made the very earth He walked on; one to be worshiped and obeyed, reaffirmed by the miracles He performed. It occurred to me that He did these deeds not only to prove Himself but also to show us the nature of God's heart. We could understand God's great love for us as we observed Jesus' love for all He encountered. Through His death on the cross, we were told this the most clearly. He gave us His all. Because of His victory over death three days later, we have eternal life through

Him. This was it. This was the assurance I'd been looking for. All I'd learned of Him now came together into a complete whole.

In a moment everything changed. I'd fallen hopelessly and completely in love with Jesus Christ.

I sat under the willow tree long after I'd finished reading, soaking up some of the truths I'd just learned. Until today, I'd been trying to figure out what to do with my life. Now I wanted to listen carefully to God's voice in my heart. Who could better direct me than the One who made me? Certainly He designed me with a purpose. I felt His hand on me as surely as if it were a physical weight. Prior to this moment, life seemed to be an endless parade of duties, hoping for a happy moment among them. No more. I just wanted to discover all God had for me to do.

This made me see Uncle Charles in a new light. I felt that he was trying to be good to please God. Now I saw that it was just the opposite. He was pleased with God and knew that God had accepted him and so it drove him to be good. This realization took a great load off my shoulders. Always discontent with my life, I became aware that as I knew God better, I would be better.

I watched in wonder as an ant crawled up my sleeve. What an intricate creature, pursuing its tasks in life with vigor. And the squirrel, so busily preparing a nest for her babies, swishing her tail as if to announce that no created thing could rival the beauty of it. Out of the corner of my eye, I saw a large hen strutting across the yard as if she owned it. Suddenly the commonplace had become extraordinary. I knew the One who formed all this out of dust! What an honor.

Pulling myself out of my lofty thoughts, I realized it was time to help Fay with dinner. The trouble with great discoveries is that they are often lost in everyday life. I couldn't stand to lose this one, so I'd have to find a way to carry it with me into the mundane. I'd have to figure out a way to love Jesus while peeling potatoes, stitching clothes, washing dishes, and weeding the garden. I knew that's what I really wanted - a way to love Jesus in everything I do.

I picked up my Bible and headed for the kitchen. Even Fay noticed a difference in my demeanor as I hummed to myself, working twice as hard as I usually do. When the men came in, I could barely contain myself. As we sat down for the meal, I asked Uncle Charles if I could pray for our meal. Surprise mingled with pleasure as he nodded his approval. I refused to look at Fay for fear that she would say something to disapprove and annihilate my newfound joy.

"Dear Lord, we thank you for the many blessings you shower upon us. Thank you for Fay's wonderful ability to cook and for Uncle Charles providing so much abundance for us. Thank you for John, and how his hard work helped to bring us all this food." I'd been speaking excitedly, full of enthusiasm. Now my voice grew softer. "But most of all we thank you for sending Jesus Christ to us. Thank you for opening my eyes to who He is. Thank you for the new adventure you've given me in life." I paused and opened my eyes, then remembered I was supposed to do something else. I quickly added, "In Jesus' name, amen."

When I lifted my head, a broad smile covered Uncle Charles' face. John looked bewildered and Fay seemed shocked. I chose to keep my gaze on Uncle Charles for the moment. "So," he began as he cut his meat, "anything special you want to talk about Rachel?"

"I spent the morning reading the book of John, Uncle Charles. I understand now what you were talking about. I feel like I know Jesus in a whole new way now."

"And so you do, my dear, and so you do," he nodded in complete understanding.

We both realized this wasn't the time and place to talk about it, so we fell silent and let Fay and John pick up the conversation on another subject. However, I noticed that at least once in the meal that Uncle Charles couldn't contain himself. He caught my eye and winked.

6

LARS SOWDERS

Spring coasted into summer. The purple irises along the path withered away, replaced by rainbow colored phlox. The light green of the leaves and grass changed to the deep green of early summer. We'd been here two months, some of the happiest times of my life.

Uncle Charles' friends from church were wonderful. They invited us often to dinner, and we returned the favor. Soon Fay and I felt as if we'd always lived here. A distinguished looking gentleman by the name of Arthur began visiting us regularly. He was a reserved man, which added to his attractiveness. It's easy to put one's confidence in a quiet person since there seems to be so much simmering under the surface. If a person thinks before he speaks, his comments seem wiser than one who constantly lets you know what's on his mind. As the book of Proverbs says, "Even a fool is thought to be wise if he is silent." Arthur, however, was anything but a fool.

Of particular interest to all of us was Arthur's work installing telephones in the area. I'd heard much about the talking wire, even knew someone who had used one in the city, but found it amazing that it was coming to a small town like Wesley. I wondered what it would be like to ring Helen on the wire to see how she's doing, or how helpful it would be for her to call the doctor when one of her children was sick. What would it be like to talk to my friends in Missouri, or to my sister in Montana? It was almost too much to imagine.

Always after these visits from Arthur, he and Fay would take long rides in the country. Fay didn't discuss it much with me, but she wrote Emily to tell her that we wouldn't be coming in the fall, which suited me. Happier than I'd ever been, my faith was growing like a seedling that branches out in all directions when it is given light and water.

Since we weren't going to Montana, I decided to carry out my plans to take in sewing jobs. Uncle Charles and his friends spread the word for me and soon I was getting customers from all over the countryside.

Ordinarily I stayed very busy, but during a lull I decided to make a dress for myself with some fabric I'd brought from Missouri. I'd been learning to listen to God's whispers to me, and as soon as I laid the fabric out, I knew as clearly as if He'd said it that I was supposed to make a dress for Helen instead. She was close to my size, which would make it easy to surprise her.

I'd continued visiting Helen regularly with Uncle Charles, but had never met her husband. I began to wonder if he even lived there anymore or if he'd abandoned his needy family. We'd invited Helen to church with us, but she'd only come once. Convinced that she felt self-conscious about her shabby clothes, I worked on this dress with great pleasure. Not only would she feel free to come to church, but she'd feel beautiful as well.

The fabric was blue polished cotton. I had some mother of pearl buttons I'd been saving and a lace collar that I'd tatted, which I placed on the fabric now, to see how they would look together. As always, I was able to envision the finished product, seeing Helen's vivid blue eyes shine in reflection of the fabric. As I got to work on it, I never enjoyed a project more.

It took longer than I'd hoped because I kept being interrupted by customers, but I finally finished it about a month after I'd started. Putting the last stitch in, I felt so anxious to take the dress to Helen that I set off by myself in the wagon, not wanting to wait until Uncle Charles finished his chores.

Climbing out of the wagon, I lifted the dress high to avoid the mud that perpetually surrounded the Sowders' home. Holding the dress crumpled next to me with my left hand, I knocked with my right. As soon as the door opened, I swept in, "Helen, I want you to come to church again with us on Sunday."

Her eyes had lit up when she saw me, but now her face fell. "I don' know, Miss Rachel. I don' think I quite fit in there."

"I know how you felt last time, so I brought you this." I let the fabric fall across my arm, revealing the lace, the buttons and the delicate tucks stitched into the bodice. Helen started to reach toward the exquisite fabric then pulled her hand back to wipe it on her apron. Shaking her head, she said, "That's so nice of ye, but I just couldn't wear it. I might ruin yur lovely dress."

"It's not mine, Helen. I made it for you." I held the dress up to her as I wrapped her into a hug. "I know you will look beautiful in it." Helen's small frame shook in my arms and I pushed away to see if she was laughing or crying. There were tears on her face, but hiccupy laughter vibrated through her delicate features.

At the sight of the dress, the children gathered around, all anxious to touch the clean, fresh fabric. Treating them as sternly as I ever had, I authoritatively announced, my finger wagging, "No one touches this dress but your mother." I gently shoved Helen behind the screen to try it on then turned to the little ones to undo the sternness of my voice. Giggles soon filled the air as each one responded to my attention, except for baby Beth who slept through it all, giving credence to the saying "sleeping like a baby".

When Helen stepped from behind the screen, Howard announced, "Pretty Mama", while the younger ones chimed in their echo of his opinion. I moved over to straighten the collar when the door flew open and banged against the wall. The children had begun laughing and chattering again, but now they became as silent as death, except for Beth who began wailing from being abruptly awakened.

A large man stepped in and slammed the door shut again. Not only was he tall, but extremely broad-shouldered as well. His hair was a nice shade of brown but looked rumpled and dirty. In spite of an unkempt beard, he had a handsome face. I could hardly stand to look at him, though, because of his steel-like eyes. His gaze felt like it burned a hole right through me. Cold chills ran up and down my back as I stood perfectly still, waiting.

"Hello, Lars," Helen ventured as she attempted to comfort Beth.

Lars tore his eyes away from me to glance at Helen. As soon as he looked away, I felt as if I'd been released from a stranglehold, but soon he was staring at me again. "Who's she?" he said in a soft voice that nevertheless communicated rage. It would have been better if he'd actually yelled, rather than use that terrifying voice.

"This is Rachel Scott, Lars. She's Charles Bradbury's niece; she's come to..." but he interrupted her, having all the information he wanted for the moment. "Where'd ya get that dress?" His voice now rose to a loud growl.

"That's what I was tryin' to tell ye, Lars. Rachel brought it over as a gift to me." Helen was trying to smile but it was a feeble attempt.

Lars' eyes now became narrow slits. I wondered how he could even see out of such a small opening. "We don' need no charity from you." He nearly spit as he spoke and I could smell the liquor that permeated his clothes and breath. "Go on home to yer nosy uncle and leave my wife be. She ain't got no time nor place to wear such a fancy get-up."

My fear turned to anger. "It's not charity. It's a gift for a friend, and ..." I would have gone on but I caught Helen's look of terror out of the corner of my eye and stopped. Clearly she was pleading me to let it drop, so I changed my approach. "I'm sorry. I didn't mean to argue with you. I hope we can meet again under more pleasant circumstances. I want to be a friend, not cause trouble in your family." I dropped my head in humility, the way a wild horse does when another has subdued it, and slipped quietly out the door.

I pressed my ear to the door, but could not hear anything, so I finally decided to get back into my wagon and head home. It was an awful moment, leaving Helen there with that man, but I didn't know what else to do. On the way home, my emotions screamed for justice in this unfair situation, and I fought hatred for this man that I'd just met. I sought out Uncle Charles as soon as I got home and relayed the whole story.

He shook his head in admonition. "Don't go there again without me, Rachel. I should have warned you about him. He's a dangerous man."

"Helen shouldn't be left there with him then. We've got to get her out of there."

"She's his wife, Rachel. What can we do?"

I nodded in frustration, but felt that I'd want to kill him if he were my husband. Of course, I couldn't tell Uncle Charles that, but it's the way I felt just the same. "Do you think we should still try to pick her up for church on Sunday?"

Uncle Charles sat quietly for a moment, and then nodded, "Yes, I think we should. From my past experience with Lars, he's usually so drunk he's forgotten what he's said from one minute to the next. Let's try it, anyway."

I prayed for Helen all week, and practically held my breath when we pulled up to her door on Sunday morning. When Uncle Charles knocked at the door, Helen looked at him in relief. "I was so afraid you wouldn't come. I got the kids all cleaned up. Would you mind waiting while I change? I didn't want to put the dress on until the last minute."

Praising God with all my heart, I jumped down from the carriage and went in to help get the kids out of the house so Helen could change in peace. When she emerged, she looked glorious, the rare smile on her face transforming her normally plain appearance more than the dress did.

As she said, the children were as clean as I'd ever seen them. She'd even taken the time to patch some of the rips in their clothes. They were surprisingly handsome when their hair was slicked down and their faces clean. I felt pleased from the top of my head to the tip of my toes. When Helen settled next to me in our now very full carriage, I asked her what had happened after I left. "Oh, nothin' much. He'd just come home to raid my money jar. I never know what he does with the money. I haven't seen him since." She said this with a look of perfect contentment on her face, but I was horrified. What a poor excuse for a husband. But I wouldn't say anything to burst the look of serenity that now covered her face.

I've never experienced a better Sunday morning. Helen listened to the sermon easily because she did not feel disapproving eyes on her and because Uncle Charles and I could help keep the children quiet. Fascinated with the little doodles I drew for them on a pad of paper I'd brought, they seemed to be rather in awe of their surroundings so they behaved themselves. The singing of the hymns, quite vigorous in this church, was their favorite part, bringing curiosity and wonder to their eyes.

Fay stayed home to prepare a feast for us after the service. When we walked in the house, the smell of roast beef and gravy permeated every nook and cranny. The children stuffed their mouths full of her fluffy biscuits and last year's grape jelly that we'd brought from Missouri. After dinner the littlest children napped. Uncle Charles and Fay visited with Helen, while I took Howard, who was four, and Henry, who was five, outside. We played "Ring Around the Rosy" and I taught them the finger play for "Here's the Church, Here's the Steeple."

Being with Helen's children did an amazing amount of good for me. I'd never been around children much and had always feared that I wouldn't have patience with them. It's odd that such a wild bunch as these five little ones would begin to create a desire in me to love a child. They also exposed me to the heartache of having children since I saw them often in their worst moods, but instead of scaring me, this challenged me.

In the middle of our play, Henry suddenly folded his arms in an obstinate manner. "These're baby games. I don' wanna play baby games."

"What do you want to play, Henry?"

"I wanna play 'robbers'. Me an' Howard'll tie you up and 'scape with all the money from the bank."

His answer threw me off guard. I began to give him all the moral reasons I could think of as to why this wouldn't be a good game. I decided to change tactics when I saw his eyes narrow into slits, just as his father's had. My heart beat a little quicker and I said, "All right. Let's race. I bet I can run faster than you can. Last one to get to that tree is a rotten egg."

Henry took off in a streak. Howard looked wide-eyed after him and began to run as fast as his little chubby legs would carry him. I had to run my hardest to catch up with Henry. We declared it a tie between Henry and me, while I cheered that Howard came in second. Howard was pleased but Henry wanted to race again. We raced until he beat me because I got tangled in my skirts. It was the first smile I'd ever seen on Henry's face.

I'd never felt wearier when Uncle Charles finally packed them into the carriage and took them home, but I had a new desire to break into Henry's world. It seemed most important that he not grow up to be like his father. I sank into a chair inside and sipped some tea, thinking about what to do. I certainly couldn't race him every time I saw him. I thought of the boys back home in Bevel who used to form a game of baseball every chance they got, and a seed of a thought took root in my mind.

7

LET THE GAMES BEGIN

When Uncle Charles came home from delivering the Sowders to their sad abode, I immediately began to expand my ideas about Henry. "Uncle Charles, we've only been to a few baseball games this summer. Don't you think we could go every week?"

"When did you get to be such a baseball fan, Rachel?"

"It's not me; it's Henry. He's going to turn out just like his father unless he finds a creative way to expend his energy. I thought if we took him weekly to the baseball games that he might take an interest in the sport."

"What an excellent idea! I'll ask Helen about it the next time I see her."

Helen, of course, readily agreed to our plan. She had already feared that Henry was heading toward a rebellious future, so we picked Henry up for the next game and headed into town.

The first week just Uncle Charles and I went with Henry. Soon our number grew to include John, Fay, and Arthur as well. These outings turned out to be the highlight of the summer. I learned that by doing things for others, we often enjoy life more in the process.

Even more important, Henry loved baseball. After we'd attended several games, John carved him his own bat and Uncle Charles bought him a ball. During any visit we made to his home after that, we found Henry practicing with his bat and ball. He taught Howard to pitch to him, remaining remarkably patient when his balls went in the wrong direction, which was most of the time.

Besides the good that came from Henry's interest in baseball, I loved seeing John's attitude toward the Sowders slowly change. John had always enjoyed baseball, which naturally drew him to Henry's budding interest. He still grumbled about Uncle Charles spending too much time helping them, but he seemed to be saying it out of habit rather than conviction.

Henry had a winning way about him. An intense child, adults found it easy to admire him. As he found interests to pour his tenacity in to, his commendable qualities began to stand out. John noticed this, encouraging Henry's budding character every chance he got.

As Henry's skill in baseball grew, the nature of his play changed from destructive to constructive. Rarely did he pretend to rob or kill people any more. Perhaps he simply didn't have time for it because he was absorbed in becoming a good ballplayer, at least when we were around to pitch a straight ball. I'd never seen such discipline in a young child. Surely that was a quality that God could use in many ways. I began to pray intently for Henry, that he would have good models to help him mold his life in the best possible direction.

Since we attended the games regularly, I began to recognize the players of the Wesley team. The catcher made the biggest impression on me. His dark brown hair lay in waves and his walnut-colored eyes twinkled in a familiar way, especially when he smiled. I felt that I'd seen that smile before, although I couldn't place where. He noticed that Henry always had his nose pressed to the fence during the games so he gave him a penny candy from his pocket each week. Henry couldn't wait to see him, as much in pride at knowing one of the players as in receiving the candy. I had to admit that my heart skipped a few beats as well when he'd come by, although his attention was always for Henry and not for me. After this had been going on for a few weeks, I finally asked Uncle Charles who he was.

"Ah, that's Tory Hampton. I don't know him very well, but I do know his parents, Thomas and Clara. Thomas is one of the finest men I've ever known. I've never heard him say a bad word against anyone." This information pleased me a great deal although I didn't understand why it should. I began to look forward to going down to the fence with Henry just so I could see Tory smile.

As we spent a lot of time each week going to and coming from the games, I told Henry Bible stories to help pass the time. I found he loved the Bible heroes such as David, Samson, Daniel, Paul, and of course, Jesus himself. Henry had an incessant desire for power and these men certainly were the most powerful he'd ever encountered. I wondered if he comprehended what these people stood for, that they lived wholeheartedly for the Lord. Were they merely exciting people or did the message of their lives break through to his young mind? I wanted Henry to understand so much more but decided not to push him. Not only would he have refused to listen, but he would have lost his love for the Bible stories. I decided it was far better for him to have a good feeling about the book even if it was a one-sided knowledge of it. If he remained interested, maybe he'd want to know what else it contained as he grew older.

I made a game of memorizing Scripture whenever possible. I took short verses and made up a simple tune to them or repeated a verse over and over in a playful way. I even tried pitching the baseball to him saying a word with each throw. If he began to act annoyed with me, I quit immediately and saved the verses for another time.

We all felt a little disappointed when the long summer days grew shorter and the cold nip of autumn bit the air. At the last game of the season, I wondered what would occupy Henry's life now. Fay came up with a solution for the time being. We invited him to help with the canning. At first he objected to this as women's work, but when

Uncle Charles offered to pay him, he changed his tune. He had his eye on a baseball mitt.

8

DAYDREAMS AND BUSINESS

Fall is a tremendously busy time on a farm. We spent our days packing away stores for the winter. Pausing a moment to observe the activity around me, we truly did look like a bunch of squirrels gathering acorns. I never minded this because I always felt fortunate for a good harvest. We would eat well this year. My only disappointment was the pumpkins. A pest had eaten the plants away until they looked like an intricate lace pattern, but did not have the strength left to bear any fruit. I hoped Uncle Charles would be able to buy some in town so that we'd have a couple of pumpkins this fall. An entire year without pumpkin pie even once was hard to face.

The most diligent work of the year came at harvesting time. Uncles Charles planted much of his land in oats to provide for his livestock. Forty men traveled from farm to farm, waiting their turn to have the steam engine harvest their crop. Weather permitting, the job would be finished in one day. As our turn drew near, Fay and I began baking bread and pies to feed the hungry crew. The day they arrived, we rose at three o'clock in the morning to fry bacon, eggs, and potatoes. As we were preparing the pancakes, teams of horses pulling racks and grain wagons began filling the barnyard. Finally the huge steam engine woke the farm with its billowing cloud of smoke and grinding gears, sounding like a great ogre about to devour its prey, which in a way it would do. The animals acknowledged its presence with oinks, squawks, moos and baas. I'd never seen such excitement, which took away the sting of all the hard work.

The yard was covered with sawhorse tables and plank benches, which the men now converged upon. Fay, Uncle Charles, John, and I served them as they consumed huge quantities of bacon, over one hundred pancakes, eighty potatoes, and fifty eggs, contributed by friendly neighbors. Never have I seen so much food go so rapidly, reminding me of a flock of locusts denuding a tree.

As soon as the men finished, we began the massive clean up. Every plate, pan, and utensil in the household as well as the numerous borrowed ones had to be washed. I felt sick to my stomach as I dumped buckets full of bacon grease into the larder. Soon the neighboring women would arrive to help with the noon meal. My spirits lifted as they brought dish after dish overflowing with food seasoned with cheerful gossip and encouraging hugs.

Henry and Howard arrived about nine o'clock with their old white horse, Grant, pulling their worn wagon. The young boys handled their responsibilities well, used to shouldering more than their share of the work around home. We filled half a dozen water jugs, wrapped in rags to keep them cool, and piled them into the back of the rig. The boys diligently carried the men their drinks and were proudly a dollar richer at the end of the day.

The noon meal was easier than breakfast because "many hands make light work." However, we collapsed into bed that night exhausted, feeling as if we'd run the length of the state. Sometimes I think the women have the harder job since the invention of farm machinery.

"No rest for the weary" in the autumn, for the next day found us back at our canning. The smell was wonderful as we canned persimmons, peaches, apricots, and cherries. By mid-morning my hands looked like prunes that have passed their prime, with a few nicks taken out of them by the sharp knife. But although my hands were busy, my mind was free. I found myself thinking more and more of Tory Hampton, imagining that his smiles were really meant for me rather than Henry. I'd find myself lost in my daydreams for hours and then scold myself for such unproductive thought. I had no opportunity to see Tory now that baseball season was over. I also knew very little about him. What if he had plans to marry someone, or what if he wasn't as wonderful as I'd made him in my imagination? However, after these self-scoldings, I soon daydreamed again.

Henry proved to be the best distraction for my thoughts. He worked non-stop to help us with the canning and by the time we'd finished the last of it, he had nearly enough money to buy the baseball mitt. He begged for more jobs, so Uncle Charles hired him to stack firewood. He promised him double the money if he would do the same for his mother at home. Henry quickly agreed and became the proud owner of a baseball mitt.

During this time of employment with us, Henry turned six years of age. We invited Helen and all the children for supper, complete with one of Fay's special cakes, topped with a mixture of butter, brown sugar, and chopped nuts. As I saw his eyes shine at this special treatment, I thought of how Henry seemed so much older than his six years. He'd grown up too quickly. In fact, there seemed to be very little of the child in him. Being carefree and trusting are the hallmarks of childhood, but Henry was neither. His father had annihilated his trust, and his mother depended on him too much to give him the freedom he needed. Why did it have to be that way? I could only trust that this was part of who God wanted Henry to be. But for this one evening, it brought me pleasure to see him completely at ease.

The culmination of the continuous work of the fall was a celebration called the Fall Festival. Everyone brought specialties from their kitchens and wore their finest. Filled with eating and games during the day, the highlight was a country dance at the Coliseum, a community building that held everything from sporting events to political rallies.

My sewing business had been steady before but now it boomed. I used every spare minute in the afternoons and evenings sewing. Fay even helped me with the hemming so that I'd finish my orders in time. As a result, I purchased the finest fabric I'd ever owned to make myself a dress for the event. Indeed, I worried after I bought it that I wouldn't have time to get it made.

One of the persons who hired me to make a shirt for him was Arthur. Now, Arthur and I had a good relationship, but I could rarely get him to smile. Therefore, I couldn't resist the temptation to use the shirt as a way to play a joke on him.

I did my best on the shirt, even down to the perfect points on the collar, until I sewed on the buttons. I made each one a different shape and color from odds and ends of buttons from previous projects. I laughed to myself as I put each button on, thinking gleefully of Arthur's reaction when he saw it.

The next time Arthur graced us with a visit, I looked for an opportunity to present the shirt. It came as we relaxed after dinner. "Arthur, I finished your shirt. I'm so proud of the work I did on it. The tucks and the collar are perfect. Would you like to see it?" I could feel the corners of my mouth stretching a bit too wide as I said this.

"I certainly would, Rachel. I've seen your work and do believe it's some of the finest."

"It is, Arthur; that Rachel can do anything she puts her mind to," chimed in Uncle Charles, looking like a proud papa.

"Rachel, you didn't tell me that you completed Arthur's shirt. Why didn't you show me?" Fay looked hurt.

"I wanted to surprise you too, Fay. Here it is!"

As Arthur took it in his hands, he just stared with a bewildered expression on his face, looking for all the world like a man who's discovered a deep, black hole in his back yard. Fay, on the other hand looked shocked, as if she'd seen a murder as she gazed at the buttons, but by the time she lifted her eyes to me, she was furious. "How could you, Rachel?" I glanced away from her to Uncle Charles and could see that he, too, had a worried look on his face. Panic gripped me, closing my throat in fear that Arthur would leave our household and never return again, and that Fay would never forgive me as long as she lived. It's amazing what can flash through your mind in a few seconds.

Then I heard a low, muffled noise. Arthur had his hand over his mouth so I couldn't tell the nature of the sound, but I soon realized from the expression in his eyes that he saw the humor in my joke. Uncle Charles quickly joined the laughter, looking as relieved as if a death sentence had been lifted. Soon they both guffawed loudly. Fay stared at them dumbfounded for a moment, but soon laughed as heartily as the rest of us. In fact, when the laughter died down, she offered to sew the proper buttons on the shirt to save me time. Arthur surprised us both by saying, "I don't know. I kind of like it this way. You may have started a new style, Rachel." I felt a warmth flood through me with a new affection for this man my sister found so appealing. And do you know, he wore it that way to the Fall Festival and got more comments on it than any other garment I'd made, which may not be a compliment to my ability.

After Arthur left, Fay came to me and squeezed my hand. "I'm sorry for my initial reaction to the buttons, Rachel. I worry too much, I know, but I sure do care for Arthur." Fay then squeezed my hand more firmly as she adopted a stern expression, "All I ask is that next time you warn me a little first." I suddenly felt an overwhelming love for this sister of mine, who had basically given up her life to raise me. I hugged her close and whispered, "I love you, Fay, and I promise to recruit you to help me in my practical jokes in the future, especially when they involve Arthur." I pulled her back to arm's length and added, "I like him Fay. At times I've thought he wasn't good enough for you, and I think I fear losing you to him, but today helped. He's a good man." She looked a wee bit uncomfortable, turning quickly to clean up the dishes.

My words made me face why I'd been feeling such mixed emotions about Fay and Arthur. It'd been the two of us for so long, I'd almost forgotten things would ever change. Since she had raised me, it was like watching a parent fall in love, but one that would leave me behind in the process. I didn't want to be left alone and began to feel angry with God for allowing it to happen so soon. Of course, Fay was twenty-nine, so she'd been patient beyond belief. There'd been a traveling salesman years ago who asked her to marry him, but she refused. I feel certain now that it was because of me, causing a new wave of guilt to flood over me for my selfishness.

All of this contemplation brought me back again to Tory. Perhaps he would be at the Fall Festival.

9

THE FESTIVAL

I finished my dress in time for the Fall Festival only because Fay took some of my daily duties for me. When I tried it on, I felt adult and elegant; both rare feelings for me. The dress was blue dimity, the color of the sky on a clear fall day. It had a high lace collar and large sleeves that puffed to the elbow and then fit tightly to my wrist, also edged in lace. The bodice had eight little tucks in the front that ended a few inches above the waist. The sash around my waist was two inches wide and tied in the back, just above the bustle. The skirt of the dress was very full so I had great fun twirling around the room watching it spin gracefully around me, the way I had often done as a little girl. Something about dress-up occasions took me back to childhood.

As Fay and I helped each other groom for this great event of the year, I marveled at how beautiful she looked. Her dark green satin dress perfectly suited her dignified look. I couldn't help wishing that I would have someone to escort me to the festival as Fay had Arthur. I didn't begrudge her though. She'd waited a long time for a man to enter her life.

So when Arthur came to pick up Fay in his carriage, I tried not to feel disappointed that Uncle Charles, John, and I would arrive in the buckboard with the entire Sowders clan. I sat in the front with Uncle Charles and Helen while John sat in the back with the children. I didn't offer to help entertain them this time. I didn't even feel like telling Henry Bible stories or holding baby Beth. The closer we came to town, the more resentful I began to feel because of my circumstances. I knew I should discuss my feelings with Uncle Charles and that he would help me gain a proper perspective, but Helen was sitting next to us, so I said nothing. I have to admit, I rather enjoyed my resentment at this point and wasn't willing to give it up. I determined to make the best of it when we arrived and not to spend the entire day with the Sowders.

It was easy to get lost in the crowd after our arrival. The afternoon activities were all outside so I was thankful that the weather was mild and balmy. The contagious excitement felt like opening day at the circus. Everyone wore smiles as the town square came alive with color and commotion. Children laughed and skipped in anticipation, crowding around the many games planned for them. I noted their joy, but stayed far from them, aware that my dress needed to stay perfect for the dance this evening. The adult women busily arranged the many dishes that everyone brought, while the men discussed politics and crop yields. I noticed that many people my age were listening to a barbershop quartet, so I decided to meander that way. As I walked nearer, I recognized one of my favorite friends from church.

"Sarah Mae, you look radiant!" An attractive girl from a wealthy family, Sarah Mae always knew the right thing to say and do, yet never lorded her station in life over me, which attracted me to her all the more. Today she was breathtaking in billows of cream-colored gauze over satin, making her look as if she were floating.

"So do you, Rachel. I thought you would never get here. Isn't this just as grand as I told you it would be? The hardest part is not eating too much so that we can still dance tonight."

We said all this in whispers so as not to disturb those listening to the quartet, so we now gave our attention to the singing. I felt terribly glad to have found Sarah Mae.

By the time they finished the number they were performing, my spirits had lifted by their gay tunes, and I began to think more about the dance. "I'm so glad we can spend the evening together at the dance, Sarah Mae."

"Oh, didn't I tell you, Rachel? Ben Watson asked if he could escort me to the dance tonight. Isn't that wonderful?" Her rosy complexion shone with excitement.

"Yes, of course, it is." I managed to force the words past my vocal cords even though my throat had just gone so dry that I could hardly swallow. At that moment, Mary, a close friend of Sarah Mae's, came close to share her excitement about an upcoming race her brother was in. I was thankful for the distraction so that she couldn't see the disappointment that had been impossible to hide.

The afternoon flew by as we watched various types of races from foot to horse, saw examples of paintings and stitchery, and ate samples of numerous delicacies. When it was time for the meal, I understood what Sarah meant about eating too much. I'd never seen so much food presented in such an attractive manner. To my delight, there were plenty of pumpkin breads and pies. All that abundance put everyone in a cheerful mood. Even Helen chatted non-stop, which was unusual for her.

"Isn't it great to be alive and know God loves ye, Rachel?"

"Mmm, yes it is, Helen."

"Ye don't seem to be yerself today. Is anythin' wrong?"

"No, Helen, everything's fine." I said this harshly as a parent would shush a child. Helen looked at me in bewilderment and I felt ashamed.

By now I was thoroughly miserable. I'd managed to drive everyone I cared about away from me, and I knew my annoyance revolved around the dance that would be taking place in a short while. The tower of anticipation I'd felt for weeks crumpled into a waste heap of disappointment. I was beginning to wish I hadn't come, when I felt a tap on my shoulder. "Well, if it isn't my angel from heaven."

I whirled around and turned bright red as I realized it was the young man from the train, dashing in a dove gray suit. "But you didn't get off at the Wesley station. What are you doing here?" I managed to squeak out.

"Ah, life is too interesting to spend in one dull town like this one. I just show up for the excitement." His eyes shone and his mouth turned up just slightly, making him look mysterious, as if his presence would magically cause things to happen. I don't think I'd ever seen a more attractive man. Just looking at him made me all jittery and excited, like a child who has just seen a toy she desperately wants.

"But you must have a home." This time my words came out clearly, confidently.

He smiled more broadly now. "Wesley's my home all right, at least where I was born and raised. My family has now risen above such dismal circumstances, however. My pop is a salesman of the new motorized farm machinery. I help him, which is why I was traveling when we so delightfully met in the railcar." As he said this, he gently lifted my hand to his mouth, brushing his lips ever so slightly across my fingers, making me feel like the queen of Sheba. "Rachel, isn't it? Rachel Scott, I believe."

I was impressed. "How can you remember? It was so long ago,"

"Now, how could I forget such blue eyes and auburn hair as yours?" He let go of my hand and traced a finger on my cheek. "I've thought a lot about Rachel Scott since the day we met," he whispered as he leaned close to me.

I had a terrible feeling I should retreat as quickly as possible, but I thought of my dim prospects for the dance and felt compelled to stay. Besides, I'd never been given attention like this and I liked the jittery feeling it gave me, almost like I was getting away with stealing cookies out of the jar when no one was looking. It felt like I was in a universe of my own making, so it startled me when the pastor of the Congregational Church welcomed us and opened the evening in prayer. The violins, mandolins, and flutes began a lively tune that made my heart skip like a lamb released from the confines of a stall into an open field.

The handsome man next to me bowed gallantly. "May I have the pleasure of this dance?"

"I don't even know your name," I objected ever so slightly.

"I am Garvin Pierce, your devoted servant. Now will you dance with me?"

I giggled at this debonair introduction and gladly took his outstretched hand as he led me to the dance floor. He turned out to be as skillful and graceful dancer as I'd ever seen. Never had I enjoyed dancing more, feeling as if I were a butterfly with wings as I flitted around the room. Garvin was also a complete gentleman with manners of gold. However, during the waltzes he held me a bit too close.

As we rested between dances, I noticed that Tory Hampton was not five feet from me. I hadn't thought of him for hours, so it startled me to realize that my heart skipped a beat when I caught sight of him. To my disappointment, he was engaged in conversation with a delicate looking blond woman. Suddenly he looked up at me, smiling brightly, just as I'd imagined him doing a thousand times. Instead of walking over to me and asking me to dance as he'd done in my dreams, he turned back to the frail beauty beside him, resuming his conversation.

"Rachel, Rachel, what are you staring at?"

"Nothing Garvin," I sighed. "Nothing at all."

"Tell you what. Let's get out of here. Would you like to have a ride on my motorized bicycle?"

"On your what?" My disappointment with Tory thudded to the ground as curiosity overwhelmed me.

"My motorized bicycle. One of my pop's presents. Come on, I'll show you." Garvin took my arm and led me towards the doorway.

"I should tell Uncle Charles first."

"Nah, we'll be gone just a minute."

The motorized bicycle looked just like a normal bicycle except fatter with engine parts attached. It seemed ridiculous to me to put a motor on a bicycle and I was sure I wouldn't like the noise. Yet I couldn't help but be curious about the contraption. Pandora's Box came to mind and I wondered if it was shaped like a bicycle.

"Come on. Get on."

"Is it safe?"

"Sure, you have nothing to worry about. You'll feel like you're riding on the wind."

As Garvin cranked the engine, I climbed on but had to sit side saddle because of my dress, pulling it tightly around my legs to keep it from getting caught in the spokes. The tremendous noise only added to the excitement as we took off with a jerk, forcing me to throw my arms around Garvin to keep from falling off.

"Isn't this great?" Garvin's smile covered his whole face as he turned to look at me, causing a shudder to go through me. I thought of the warm, accepting smile Tory gave me back at the dance. Garvin's smile was consuming. Instead of Pandora's Box, I now thought of *The Fox and the Crow*. However this fox didn't want to eat just my cheese but me as well. I knew I'd made a mistake and that I could do nothing about it now.

I became even more worried when he headed for the creek. He stopped right in the middle of the bridge. "Now wasn't that the most excitement you've ever had?" I felt myself simmering as he stared at me coolly.

"It was terrible. I've never been bounced around so much in my life, and why did you start with such a jerk?"

Garvin's laugh was loud and brash. "So I could feel your arms around me, of course," he crooned as he leaned toward me, pulling me into his close embrace. I tried to push him away, but he was too strong. "How dare you! Take me back to the dance immediately."

Garvin looked down at me with the slight smile that had seemed so mysterious a short while before and now looked sinister, like a wolf about to swallow his prey. "Why should I do that? I have you all to myself here." He ran his hand through my hair, pulling out a few of the carefully placed pins.

For the first time I began to be truly frightened. No one knew I was here; what could I do? I then remembered what I'd chosen not to do all day...talk to God. I sent up a quick prayer, begging His forgiveness and asking Him to rescue me now. I don't know what I expected Him to do, but I trusted Him fully.

In spite of this feeling, I was startled to hear another voice ring out from the shadows. "Garvin, leave her alone!" I strained in the growing darkness to see who it could be. As the voice moved out of the trees into the moonlight on the bridge, I was shocked to see Tory and another man approaching.

Even more surprised than I, Garvin stepped back so quickly that he stumbled into his bicycle causing the whole thing to come down with a crash, with him on top of it. Tory and his friend began to chuckle. "Serves you right, Garvin! Maybe you won't bother sweet young girls anymore." As Garvin struggled to get off his bicycle, he slipped back down again, this time smearing a great line of grease down his perfectly tailored coat. I'd been silent but began to nervously giggle. Soon we were all laughing out loud, except Garvin, who now looked like the hunted fox instead of the hunter. As he climbed on his motor vehicle and roared away, I thought of Georgie Porgie.

Turning back to Tory I asked, "How did you know we were here?"

"I saw you leave with Garvin and knew he would be up to no good. I attended school with him for years and he was always devising a way to get the girls alone. I knew you'd be sorry you went with him, so Paul and I decided to follow you. It wasn't too hard with the pinging noise that motor made."

"I'm extremely grateful to you both. I greatly misjudged his character. To be honest, I never liked him in the first place. I don't know what made me go with him." I said this with a pang of guilt as I thought of the selfish way I'd lived the day.

"By the way," Tory continued, "I know you're the girl who always brought Henry to the games, but we've never been introduced. I'm Tory Hampton and this is Paul Sherman." Paul tipped his hat politely to me although he didn't say a word.

"I'm Rachel Scott. I'm living with my uncle, Charles Bradbury. I believe he knows your parents, Tory."

"Oh yes, we've known Mister Bradbury for a long time." I could see the twinkle in his eyes was back. Where had I seen those eyes before? They gave me goose bumps from my head to toe. "Which reminds me, he'll be worried if he finds you missing. We'd better get back to church."

Tory helped me into the family's carriage and we chatted merrily as we rode back to church. God had certainly rescued me and given me more than I deserved. I remembered a verse in the Psalms in which David said "the goodness of God leads to repentance." I cleared my heart before Him and arrived carefree at the dance.

10

FOOD FOR THE SOUL

The following afternoon, I found myself pouring out my story to Uncle Charles. He'd noticed I was gone for a while from the dance, but assumed I was with some friends so he hadn't worried. Now his eyebrows arched, his eyes squinted, and his mouth pursed in concern as I recounted the evening's activities. I also explained that I had wanted to talk to him about my frustrations with being with the Sowders family.

"Rachel, I had no idea all this had been going on. I would gladly have listened to your feelings if you had drawn me aside after we arrived. I understand that you are young and that you get tired of being responsible for other people. Not that I am excusing your behavior; think how Helen must feel. She's not much older than you."

"I know, Uncle Charles." I thought that if there was a mirror around, I'd be able to see the misery on my face. I certainly felt it to the core of my being. "I feel awful about it now." But there was something stubborn in me too that didn't seem totally wrong. "Perhaps it wasn't wrong for me to want to spend some time independent of them," I began as I searched his face for any form of approval. "But it was my attitude of self-pity that led me astray, don't you think?"

The corners of Uncle Charles mouth turned up slightly and I knew that being annoyed with me was a difficult thing for him. "Yes, I think that's a fair summation." Then, as if remembering that he was letting me off easily, he added, "Self-pity is always destructive and should be dealt with immediately. I agree; it wasn't wrong for you to want some freedom from the Sowders. If you needed time to be refreshed so that you would have the strength to minister to them further, that would be a good reason. If you only wanted rid of them because they hurt your social standing, that's a very poor reason indeed."

As he said this, I wished I didn't have such a light complexion for my face flushed once more as hot as it could be. "I'm not sure what my reasons were, Uncle Charles. Sometimes I can be so selfish." Even as the words left my mouth, I felt their truth in a new way. I began to understand how deeply my self-centeredness went, and it was awful. The weight of it felt like a hippopotamus on my shoulders.

At this worst of moments, Uncle Charles responded by putting his long arms around me, pulling me close. "It's all right, Rachel. We all have our moments of complete selfishness. As you mature, they become less and less if you are letting Him have more of your life." Then he pushed me out to arms length, still clutching my shoulders as he stared at me, the way my dog used to watch my eyes carefully when I was talking to him. "You are a splendid young woman. If I ever had a child of my own, I would want her to be just like you."

His words sunk deep into my soul like a potted flower that is wilted and longing for a good drink of water. It was as if his words were God's own, causing even my posture to improve as I stood before him. The words caught in my throat for a moment as I tried to express thankfulness for the gift he had just given me. "I'm so lucky to have you, Uncle Charles. I know you have a lot to do, but do you suppose we could spend this day together, just you and me?"

The way his face lit up was answer enough. "I think that's a splendid idea. What would you like to do?"

"I'd like to take a long walk in the country and gather an entire basket of wildflowers to put on the dining room table." Suddenly I knew that our busy fall schedule had taken a deep toll on me, and the country walk sounded lovelier than a trip to the city.

"Let's do it! I could use a day like that myself."

There is nothing quite like a walk in the fall. The weather was perfectly crisp and the trees were brilliant shades of red and yellow. I gathered bittersweet along the fence rows, clipped the milkweed pods that were just starting to open, and picked up hedge apples along the way. I've always loved the way butterflies flit around the wildflowers, particularly the wild asters. There seemed to be hundreds of them out today, working frantically to get their labors finished before winter. As we walked we sang "I Come to the Garden Alone". Always my favorite hymn, it seemed particularly appropriate to sing it out here in God's garden. Uncle Charles and I decided that He did a much better job in arrangements than we could ever do in our neatly groomed flower patches.

We soon came to a stand of trees that bid us to explore. Here I added branches of wild berries, twigs of bright, red sumac, and as many pinecones as would fit in my basket. If there were hundreds of butterflies on the wild flowers, there were thousands of lady bugs flying up from the fallen leaves as our boots rustled through them. I began sticking my foot as far under the leaves as I could, kicking them up into the air as I had as a child. Finally, we rested on a fallen log, so long there that moss had begun to grow on it, making a nice carpet to sit on. I let a lady bug crawl up my skirt and tried to count her spots.

As a child, I used to fancy that such woods were full of enchanted creatures. The many fairy tales I'd indulged in as a youngster came to life in such a place as this. Even now I felt like looking over my shoulder to see if a tree was coming to life or an elf sneaking into his treasure land under the earth. My delight in these stories increased as I came to know Christ and began to understand that another world does exist besides the one we see with our eyes now. Certainly the discoveries we make in His kingdom will be far more exciting than the best fairy tales.

"I believe this is just what you needed, Rachel," Uncle Charles spoke bringing the present world back around me. "We all do. It gives one a new perspective on life to observe God's wonders."

I simply sighed in agreement and breathed the fresh air around me.

By the time we made it back home, the sun was beginning to set. There were just a few clouds on the horizon, which captured and dispersed the vanishing sun's rays. A thousand hues of coral burst above them, giving the heavens a glorious fan of color. We finally dragged ourselves inside when the last ray of light vanished from the sky and the stars shone in their brilliance.

My wildflower bouquet lasted for weeks. Each time I looked at them, it brought back to me the refreshment of that day. As my duties resumed they were lighter, for my mind was lifted above them. I determined to take such days any time in the future when my burdens seemed too heavy.

11

WINTER FROLICS

The autumn days were over all too soon and the winter snows began, covering the brown earth with a frosting of white. There was a lot more snow in Wesley than there had been in Missouri, but everyone seemed to enjoy it more here. I particularly relished the sleigh rides, which I found endless excuses to take.

When I offered to go to town for Uncle Charles to buy supplies, he graciously trusted me with his team of horses and the sleigh. I'd grown to love his horses, Patches and Lady, and they seemed to love me too. I'm sure the sugar lumps I brought them had something to do with their affinity towards me. Patches was my favorite. She was a pinto with a gentle, obedient spirit, which is an admirable quality in a horse. Lady, however, was misnamed because she was anything but. She loved to display the fact that she had a mind of her own. John taught me how to firmly control the reins so that she would know that I was in command. As a result, we got along fairly well, at least enough so that Uncle Charles trusted me with her.

Therefore I took great pleasure in my ride in the bright red and green painted sleigh as I made my way towards town, the sleigh bells ringing out a rhythm that beat the best of bands. I must admit I took more turns than necessary to get there, just to enjoy a longer ride.

When I finally did make it to the general store, I found Sarah Mae there, to my delight. She lived in town so did not have the pleasure of riding in a sleigh to get here. Ah, poor girl.

"Sarah Mae, how are you? Have you been anywhere else with Ben Watson?" I asked with a smirk as I tilted my head to show my curiosity.

She returned my smile, looking pert as she leaned close to me with her answer. "As a matter of fact, he's been riding in to see me quite often." Her eyes took on a dreamy look, the way my cat looks when she's been purring. "He's a wonderful man. How can I be so lucky?"

I knew I was doing better in my attitude because I was truly happy for her rather than jealous of her. "You certainly are fortunate, Sarah Mae, and I'll add that he's found quite a treasure too." It was fun to praise Sarah Mae for she always took it thankfully without apology or embarrassment. She now laughed out loud, reminding me of the sleigh bells then quickly changed the subject.

"I almost forgot. We're all meeting in the park this Saturday afternoon for a snow party. I meant to tell you last Sunday but I forgot about it until now."

"What's a snow party?" My curiosity was high, making me feel like a bird about to swallow a worm. I hadn't been to a social event since the Fall Festival and I longed to be with others my age.

"We sled down the hill on the east side of the park, near the river. Last year some of the men poured water on it so that it became a sheet of ice. It was grand going so fast. After that we built snowmen with Dr. Watson as the judge to which one is best. This year Rev. Brown is going to do it for us."

"You do this every year?"

"We try to. It's such great fun. Many of us have been planning our snowmen for months. You'll come, won't you Rachel?"

"I wouldn't miss it." I tossed my head and flipped the edge of my coat out to emphasize my words.

I didn't dawdle on my way back to the farm after securing the supplies. I wanted to finish my sewing jobs so that I'd be free on Saturday. It's amazing how motivating one event can be.

Saturday morning dawned cold and blustery. Flurries violently slammed against the windows, shaking them in their frames. Uncle Charles said that it was out of the question that I could leave for town in such conditions. Disappointment settled over me like the drifts forming outside my window, but I tried to thank God that He knew best and look for His push in my day.

By the time I set the table for the noon meal, the wind began to die down. The flurried continued while we ate, but by the time we'd finished our dinner, they'd stopped. "Look, Uncle Charles. It's clearing up." I looked at him hopefully, feeling like a five-year-old waiting for permission to play outside.

To my disappointment he shook his head. "It's too unpredictable, Rachel. If it starts back up again, you'll be in real trouble."

I did my best to recover my emotions and helped Fay finish the dishes. By now the sun shone brightly and all trace of the evil looking clouds had vanished. Feeling foolish, I couldn't refrain from asking one more time. In fact, all I had to do was enter the parlor with a questioning smile on my face.

"Oh, all right. You can go, if John agrees to drive you," Uncle Charles said as he buried his face back in his newspaper.

I turned to John with such a bright look on my face that I knew it would be almost impossible for him to refuse me. "Well, I mi's well forget relaxin'. I'll get my coat Miss Rachel."

I went over to plaster a kiss on his cheek. "Thanks, John. I won't forget this." His grin made him look almost as if he were wagging his tail.

The ride into town made me fall in love with winter all over again. Snow clung to the branches of the trees, looking as if they were draped in satin. The muddy fields were covered with a fresh-fallen blanket of pure white, not a speck of dirt to be seen. Sculptured hills and mounds transformed the flat landscape. The roads were still unused after the storm so that our runners made the first mark. Even the animals seemed to respect the new face their world had found. The rabbits gingerly jumped across the road, as if they felt guilty for marring it.

When we arrived at the park, it was full of people. Not only people my age, but entire families turned out for the event. I found Sarah Mae amongst the rainbow of coats and ran to her.

"Isn't it grand the way the weather has changed, Rachel?" she exclaimed with outstretched arms.

"It sure is. I sang to God in my heart all the way here."

"You are such a funny girl, Rachel. Did you bring your sled?"

"No, I'm afraid Uncle Charles isn't very well equipped for such outings."

"That's all right. We have plenty. I'll just ask around to see if anyone would like to share theirs with you."

I began to look around, feeling a wee bit nervous for the first time, wondering if I would be putting anyone out, when Tory approached me. "I hear you're in need of a sled. Would you like to share mine?"

I felt as if I would stop breathing. After my embarrassing behavior at the Fall Festival, I'd given up hope that Tory would ever take an interest in me. I'm sure my answer wasn't as long in coming as it seemed to me. "I'd love to," I finally forced out, then told myself that this meant absolutely nothing and to keep my heart in check.

Tory gave me one of his winning smiles and offered his hand as we climbed the hill, sending goose bumps down my arm that had nothing to do with the winter weather. The men iced the hill again this year so that we went speeding down. I sat in front holding my skirts tightly around me to avoid getting them caught in the runners. Tory sat behind me but had to reach around me to control the ropes which steered the sled. The security I felt at that moment, I'd not felt since my father died. Tory's warmth flooded through me like a crackling fire on a cold night. I wanted the moment to last forever but of course, it didn't. All too soon, we ended in a tumble at the bottom of the hill. As he helped me up, I looked away because it was almost painful to look into his beautiful brown eyes.

After a while, the men decided that they should race down the hill. While the women waited at the bottom, the men lined up their sleds. Some of the sleds were fine store bought ones, others obviously homemade. Tory's was of the latter group, but he'd painted it brightly and polished the runners until they glowed.

There were eleven sleds in all. The first five that crossed the finish line would be allowed to race again. From that group the first two would match their skills of speed.

Sarah Mae was chosen to yell "Go!" which would start the race. The first run sent all of us into gales of laughter. Because they were trying to go so fast, the men were tipping over right and left. Only seven actually made it over the finish line. Tory, his friend Paul, and Benjamin all made it. Paul, however, was not in the first five so he was eliminated.

The second race was more serious. Only one rolled this time. My heart jumped with excitement when I realized that Tory would be one of the final two to race. Why did that matter to me? The other man was named Eddie, I learned as everyone yelled for one or the other to win. As Eddie and Tory got in their positions, I saw them playfully punch one another.

The race ended in a moment with all of us screaming at the top of our lungs. I said very little for fear of being too obvious, which made me feel slightly guilty when Tory lost by a hair. I followed the crowd over to congratulate Eddie and give Tory our condolences, although a few took the opportunity to knock Tory down into the snow and give him a good-natured pummeling. As he stood to brush the snow off, I added, "I'm sorry you lost."

"That's all right. It's tolerable to lose to your own brother. You've never met him, have you?" He looked toward Eddie, yelling, "Edward, call off your victory crowd. I want you to meet Rachel." Everyone looked toward us as Eddie slowly walked our way. I felt that time had stood still. Tory wanted me to meet his brother. He wanted it enough to let everyone in attendance know so. For the first time my heart dared to hope.

I spent the rest of the day with Tory. We worked on his plans for a snowman that he intended should look just like Theodore Roosevelt. He even brought his father's spectacles from home to place on the end of the snowman's nose and a large stick for his molded arm. It was a rather pitiful attempt and we didn't win.

John finally fetched me after spending the afternoon at the general store. Tory helped me into the sleigh, thanking me for the day. "I really think I would never have gotten those spectacles to stay on Teddy if you hadn't broadened his nose. He turned out pretty 'bully', don't you think?"

I turned my nose up as I looked over at our snowman. "Yes. I don't understand why we didn't win," I said as I glanced over at the exquisite castle that had outshined us all.

"Neither do I," he said as he winked at me. He patted my hand and gave me a parting smile which I held in my mind all the way home. I noticed that John was hiding a grin from me, but I pretended to ignore him as I looked the other way so that he couldn't see the smile refused to leave my face.

12

COURTING DAYS

Tory came to see me a couple of weeks after the snow party, bringing me peppermints and peanuts from his father's general store. I tried not to act overjoyed. A woman must keep her dignity in such situations, Fay is always telling me. So I did my best to contain my happiness, but I doubt that I was too convincing.

I always did have trouble doing what I was supposed to. When I was younger, Fay continually scolded me for leaving my bonnet off in the sun, causing my face to freckle. I liked the fresh brown spots all over my face, but she thought it was shameful.

Then there was all this business of being a lady. Even though Father wanted us to be sturdy, he still felt our behavior should be ladylike. It was fine with everyone that I climbed trees when I was younger, but now I was never to indulge in childlike or boyish behavior. Sometimes the temptation to climb a tree became so strong that I'd hike up my skirts and do it anyway when I thought no one was looking. The joys of living in the country!

Most difficult of any of these things was the fact that I was not to show a man that I was interested in him. I agree that women who flirt continually with every man they meet is disgusting, but here was a man I really cared about. I wanted him to know how delighted I was with his intentions toward me, so I'm afraid I did poorly at appearing uninterested.

Being with Tory was wonderful. He made me feel accepted; never like I needed to put on airs for him. Our relationship smacked of the truest friendship yet he excited me to the depth of my being. He enjoyed my sense of humor and I loved his consistent, steady personality.

After several such visits, Tory asked me if I would come to his home to meet his parents. On the day he was to take me, I began to grow nervous. What if they didn't approve of me? There was no way that they could know my background, which would be a strike against me in this small town where everyone knew everyone. By now I understood that the Hampton family was one of the most respected families in the area, and I was just a poor orphan from Missouri. Even I could see that I didn't talk right, with my slight accent.

Suddenly all I'd ever learned about being a lady came into play. I protected myself by being rather stiff and formal. I tried to remember all the rules Fay had drilled into me over the years. Perhaps if I remained cool, Mr. and Mrs. Hampton would be impressed.

When we arrived at the Hampton home, a large colonial structure in town, the first person we met was Eddie. Fun-loving and easy to converse with, I immediately began to relax. His good-natured ribbing toward his brother about me brought the red back to my cheeks just as we walked in the door, to my disgust. Mrs. Hampton came to greet us as soon as she heard our voices. When I saw her, I broke into a wide grin. She was the woman at the train station with the amazing eyes. That's why Tory's eyes looked so familiar to me. Hers were the first eyes I'd seen in Wesley and had stayed with me all this time. I'd liked Mr. and Mrs. Hampton from the moment I'd seen them, but would they like me?

Mr. Hampton soon joined our party, and I found my tongue tied again. His mere presence commanded respect with his gray whiskers and tall form, yet he had a warm, gentle way about him too. I could understand why Uncle Charles thought so well of him.

All went smoothly until dinner when I offered to help in the kitchen. Mrs. Hampton asked me to peel the potatoes, a simple task that I've done a thousand times before with no trouble at all. I don't know whether it was because I was nervous or if being in the kitchen with a witness threw me into chaos.

The first thing I did was cut my finger quite badly with the knife. As I bled all over the place, Missus Hampton wrapped a rag around it and told me to fill the enormous pot with water. If I could do that, she would finish the peeling. Because of the rag wrapped around my hand, I had trouble gripping the huge pot. I almost got it to the stove when it slipped from my hand and crashed to the floor. Several gallons of water went everywhere and my tears added to the general deluge.

"I'm sorry Mrs. Hampton. I should never be allowed into a kitchen. I just make a mess," I wailed, certain that she would advise her son to stay far away from me in the future.

"Nonsense, child," she said in a soothing tone, the way a mother would comfort a distraught baby, which made me feel even worse. Then she did the most wonderful thing. She began to laugh. Not just a little chuckle but a deep down belly laugh that shook her whole body. It was the perfect reaction. My tears quickly turned to laughter and we both were so hysterical that we had to hold on to the table to remain upright. When she finally got her composure again she said, "When I first met Mr. Hampton's parents, I spilled an entire pitcher of milk all over the wonderful dinner his mother made. I wanted to die. This reminded me of that moment." She shook her head at the memory and I loved her so much I wanted to hug her. "Fortunately, water is much easier to clean up than milk. Do you mind scrubbing my floor?" she asked, and the twinkle in her eyes was more beautiful than ever.

"I'd love to. I was hoping you would ask," I said with a mischievous air. I could tell she approved of my response as she handed me a rag.

The rest of the dinner proceeded without a hitch. All my fears were completely unfounded. They accepted me with open arms. I felt I was part of the family by the time we left.

As Tory and I made our way back through the ice and snow, we seemed to have a new bond. By meeting his family, I understood him better. "You are so lucky to have both your parents living."

"I guess I am. I never really thought about it before. Parents are something you take for granted."

"Their life seems so happy, as if nothing has ever gone wrong for them."

"I do think they're happy, but not because their life has been carefree. My father has had some big failures with his business in the past and they lost three children after Eddie and I were born."

"How awful! That must be the hardest thing in the world to go through."

"Yes, but they still have Eddie and me," he said with a wink. "Who could ask for more than that?"

"Do you know your parents were the first people I saw in Wesley when we arrived last spring? They were greeting a woman at the station."

"That must have been my aunt. She stayed with us for a month around that time."

"Do you also know you have your mother's eyes? When I first saw you at the baseball games, I felt I knew you because of them."

Our conversation now fell silent as Tory reached for my hand. He squeezed it tightly through my bulky mitten and held it until necessity caused him to put his hands on the reins again. The warmth of this gesture, even through all our layers, made me feel like a cat that had curled up in the sun. Nothing else Tory had done spoke so truly of his affection for me.

We parted reluctantly at the farm. I whistled all the way up the porch stairs and into the house after he could no longer see me waving. Fay scolded me for such unladylike behavior as whistling, of course, but it didn't bother me a bit.

13

FAY AND ARTHUR

One winter day when life seemed utterly monotonous, Arthur came to talk long and seriously with Uncle Charles. Arthur was close in age to Uncle Charles, and they enjoyed each other thoroughly, so this in itself was not unusual. What was out of the ordinary was the fact that Fay did not join in their conversation and that she was as restless as a fox looking for mouse. She began stirring a cake then absently left it as she stared out the window. Soon she was back at the cake, adding more eggs. I was sure there were at least five of them in the cake by now.

At long last, when the cake had been beaten beyond any reasonable time, Arthur came into the kitchen with Uncle Charles and gave Fay a tender kiss on the cheek. He then approached me and gave me a big hug. This was so out of character that I stepped back in surprise.

"How would you like a new brother-in-law, Rachel?" Arthur beamed as if he was the sun rising.

Of course, I'd expected this. "I think it would be wonderful!" Fay looked as if she would sprout wings and fly. I returned Arthur's hug politely and then hugged my sister fiercely.

"I've only one request from you, Rachel." Arthur wore a serious expression as he addressed me. "If I hire you to make my wedding shirt, you are to let Fay sew the buttons on." He then grinned like the Cheshire Cat.

"Very well," I sighed. "If you want the same old boring buttons all the way down, that's fine with me." Then I smiled mischievously, "But I'm not making any promises about the pants."

He punched me gently on the arm while Fay put her cake in the oven. I teased her about all the eggs in it and she acted put out with me, but I knew that she was as happy as she'd ever been.

After Arthur left, I began to pump Fay with questions. "How long have you two been planning this announcement?"

"Arthur asked me to marry him two days ago. I've been nearly bursting to tell you but he wanted me to wait until he could talk to Uncle Charles. I hope you'll forgive me for letting you know about it this way."

"Of course I do. Have you set a date yet?"

"I've always wanted a spring wedding. Arthur doesn't care when, just so long as it's soon. He's ready to end bachelor life as quickly as possible. We'll get married the first week of April. That will give me a month and a half to get ready. You will help me with a dress, won't you?"

"I've never made a wedding dress. I'd love to! Do you have any idea what you want?"

"Nothing too showy. I'm too old to make such a hoopla over getting married."

"That's ridiculous. You're not old and this wedding is just as important as if you were nineteen, maybe more because you've waited so patiently for this. Let's get out the patterns and see if we can design something exquisite."

A hopeful smile broke out onto Fay's face, like a child who has just been told she can go to the parade after all. As we began to look through patterns and combine this sleeve with that bodice, my own fears about marriage began to surface. "What do you think it will be like to be married?"

"I don't know. I suppose over all life won't be much different than it is now. There will still be chores and meals. Of course, children will change life a great deal, but it will be comforting to have a man who loves and cares for me."

"What was our parent's marriage like? Did they love each other?"

"Yes, I think they did." Fay looked wistful, yet satisfied as she pushed her mind to remember. "Of course, there always seemed to be a lot of trouble. Nothing ever went smoothly for them, but they met it with humor and overcame their trials. Papa adored Mama. He was never quite the same after she died. You were the one he poured his affections on after that."

Her words brought a lump in my throat and for the first time I thought about what it must have been like for her at age twelve to lose her mother and have to care for me all those years.

Fay interrupted my thoughts. "Do you remember Betsy Houston, Rachel?"

"Not really. Mostly just what you told me."

"That was the saddest time of my life. Papa married her when you were tiny, mostly because he was desperate to have someone care for you. Betsy was in her early twenties. He didn't know her very well but she was from a good family. She stayed only two years, making life miserable for us. I think it was too much responsibility for her." Then Fay paused as if thinking further. "Or maybe she knew that Papa's heart was still with Mama, which wouldn't be fair to any woman. He expected her to act just like Mama, which of course, she couldn't do. She left shortly after Eugene was born and we never heard from her again. I think that's why I've been so particular about a husband. I didn't want to make a mistake like that."

Fay had shared this story with me before, but it hit me with new emotion this time, making me more thankful than ever that she now had a kind man to marry who would erase some of her past hurts. I hated feeling so melancholy so I decided to change the subject. "Do you know what I'm most worried about in marriage?"

Fay smiled like that cat that had just swallowed the canary. "Probably that you will have to grow up and act properly."

"Noo. I'm already grown up and act properly. You just refuse to recognize it."

"Hmm."

"I'm most worried because I hate to cook. What if I just get sick of it and we have to live off of dry bread crusts?"

"Cooking is just a matter of experience. I had to start as a child, you know. My first cooking effort after Mama died was a disaster. Didn't I ever tell you that story?"

"No, but I'm dying to hear it." I'm ashamed to admit it, but to hear that Fay failed at anything made me feel better.

"Papa hired a man to help him on the farm during the spring planting. Mama always fed the hired hands, so I decided to make a fine meal as she used to. It really didn't turn out too badly until I attempted the gravy. When I served it, the hired man asked if it was corn because it was so pale and lumpy. I was terribly embarrassed, but Papa never said a word, just ate it as if it were fit for a king. I think it was his encouragement that caused me to want to be a good cook. If he thought I'd done a good job, he'd say, 'Fay Marie, that was a bully meal.' That was all the praise I needed."

"That should give me hope, but what if my husband isn't as nice a Papa? Then what will I do?"

"You'll learn to keep your mouth shut, Rachel, just like I've taught you." The tender moment between sisters was over. Fay was back to being my mother.

Somehow her story made me homesick. "Fay, let's go back."

"Go back where?"

"To Bevel. Let's visit for just a week before you get married. I want to see the old farm and all our favorite places. After you get married, we'll never get back."

Fay looked at me as if I'd suggested going to the moon. "Rachel, I've only got a month and a half as it is to get ready for this wedding."

"We can work on your dress on the train and while we're visiting. I'll work night and day if you want me to. Please, let's go."

"It's a ridiculous idea." Fay said the words slowly, as if she was considering it, but then she squared her shoulders with that look of determination I've seen so many times. "No. I'm sure it's out of the question. How do you come up with these ideas anyway?"

14

HOME AGAIN

In a week we were on the train headed to Missouri. This ride was quite different from the last. The sense of purpose and meaning I'd gained in a few months had transformed me. I could see now how everything wove together to bring me to the point of seeing my need for God, and now my life was unfolding like a flower that has been exposed to sunlight after a long, dark winter.

To pass the time, I took out the one photo I had of my mother, taken shortly before she died. I remember the first time I saw it, saying to my father that she wasn't very pretty. Papa, who I knew to be kind and gentle towards me, became furious, "You little snot nose! You will never be half as good looking." I never forgot his words and thought I must be very ugly for him to say such a thing. It wasn't until recent years that I understood his anger and loved him for his loyalty to my mother.

My first glimpse of Bevel outside the window of the train sent a flood of warmth through me, like drinking hot chocolate on a cold winter day. It was a cozy feeling, the way one feels after being away from home for a long time.

Bevel's a railroad town and although not large, it does a good deal of business. It's a shipping point for almost all the hogs and cattle transported between St. Louis and Kansas City. Its bustle and activity is what drew my parents here many years ago.

We stayed with our friends, the Simpsons. They were a busy family, which was just as well because we had a lot of freedom to do as we pleased. After freshening up, we decided to go see our old farm, borrowing their buckboard and faithful old nag. On the way, we passed the schoolhouse which held almost as many memories as home. I started school when I was just four years old because there was no one to stay home with me.

School was in session, but we peeked in through the window without disturbing the students. Little had changed so the visions of days gone by flooded my thoughts. As a small child I was terrified, especially when the big, grown-up boys attended. They only came when they were not in the fields working. They obviously didn't want to be there by their attitude toward the teacher. I only had one teacher who didn't carry a gun or club for protection. I remember my horror when one particular teacher slammed Sal's head on his desk. It didn't curb his behavior much, but it made angels out of the rest of us.

Of course, there were happy moments too...lunches with my girlfriends under the big maple, playing kick-the-can, listening to Carol Ferguson recite scenes from Macbeth. These were the experiences that played most in my mind when I thought of school.

We climbed back onto the buckboard for the four more miles to our farm. It'd been a long walk when I was four years old. We had to walk by Jesse James' house on the way. He was dead by that time, but his house held awful dread for me. Papa told me that before I was born, Jesse came to look at his horses. He'd been terribly worried for Jesse simply took any horse he wanted. Papa told me with a chuckle that he'd never been so thankful for his old nags. If they'd been fine horses, he would have to pull his plow by himself.

The farm looked just the same. The family now renting it welcomed us with open arms and gave us permission to wander around. I felt a pang of guilt at my wicked thoughts toward them when they'd moved in after us.

As I wandered down to the river, always my favorite spot, I thought of my two playmates as a child. Don was a large Newfoundland and Spot, a small fox terrier. We roamed the riverbanks together, with the terrier always in the lead. He made all the decisions which neither Don nor I ever questioned.

Spot's favorite place in the summer, and therefore Don's and mine also, was a forty-acre lake near us. As Fay and I walked there now, we laughed at how I used to shoot water moccasins from the willow branches. In winter we had bonfires here and skated on the frozen pond.

Perhaps my best memory was my many walks with Papa around the farm. He always grew watermelons in the summer, which we would cut open and eat together right in the middle of the field. He loved to call me "Carrot Top" in the summer because the sun brought out so much red in my hair.

We soon had wandered everywhere we could and knew it was time to go. As pleasant as it was to remember, there was only so much reminiscing one can do at one time. After a while the memories all blend together like a concerto with too many movements. When we arrived back at the Simpsons, we heard an active political debate going on in the parlor. I never could understand the reason for debates in Missouri. All the white folks were Democrats and all the Negroes were Republicans, out of loyalty to Mr. Lincoln. A really interesting debate would be between the whites and the coloreds; that I would enjoy listening to. As it was now, the points of disagreement were so minor that I didn't even bother to listen.

I had several colored friends. Some of us white folks drove our buggies to the Negro's church just to hear them sing. I particularly enjoyed the way Mama Bryant played the piano at the services. She never needed a hymnal, only her ear for music. Her fingers flew over the keys and her foot tapped the beat, making it impossible to sit still while listening to her. Often the solos were performed without any accompaniment at all. My friend Cornelia had a powerful voice that shook the rafters. I enjoyed the freedom at these worship services which I never found at our sober church.

The second day of our visit, Fay insisted on seeing many of my parent's old friends. She made a list of four families she felt we must pay a call to. The last on the list was a couple by the names of Fred and Lettie. He, or perhaps more accurately, she, had been our landlord. I'd always thought them odd, but didn't argue with Fay. After our visit with them, I asked Fay why they were so strange.

"I'm not sure what made them so strange in the first place but didn't I ever tell you how they got married?"

"I don't know. Is it something I would like to hear?" Gossip always made me nervous because I could never look at the person the same way again.

"It's worth hearing whatever its merit. Lettie told it to Mama years ago, even bragged about it, which is beyond me."

"My curiosity is up. How did it happen?"

"Fred evidently worked for Lettie's brother, Charles, who was as well-off as she. They shared a mansion that they inherited from their father. Since it was so large, Fred stayed in the mansion with them, along with another man in their employment. Every night Lettie insisted they sit up with her late in the evening to talk. However, after an especially hard day at work, Fred and the other employee decided to draw straws so that only one would have to sit up with the "old maid" as they called her. Fred won or lost, however you look at it, and got the task. Lettie was quite pleased to have Fred to herself and showed him what a fine foot and leg she had. Fred didn't think so favorably of this until he worked out a plan. The next night he sat up with Lettie again and said he would marry her if she gave him a thousand dollars cash. She agreed to do this if he would use it to buy cattle, as she always wanted a businessman husband. He obliged, and here they are." Fay rolled her eyes and I had to admit that this story explained a lot about Fred and Lettie.

Our last day in Missouri, Fay and I decided to spend separately, seeing many of the friends who were special to each of us. The first person I wanted to see was Aunt Agnes. She wasn't my aunt by blood but I fell to calling her that soon after we became acquainted.

The worst part about leaving Missouri had been parting with Aunt Agnes. In her seventies now, I'd first met her seven years ago when she asked around town for someone to help her with the housework. Papa told me about it and I agreed, rather reluctantly, to spend my Saturday mornings helping her for a small wage. Agnes was a rather tall woman, but frail and delicate. She was in good health but had taken a bad fall and broken her hip. Being a determined sort, she now moved slowly with the help of a built-up shoe. Still housework was difficult so she needed my help.

Aunt Agnes was a lady through and through. She dressed in the most feminine fashion. All her dresses were made from the same pattern but varied in fabrics and trim. She confided in me once that one of the worst things about breaking her hip was that she must now wear these horrid, sturdy shoes. Prior to that time, her favorite shoes were delicate slippers.

In spite of her proper ways, she was fun-loving and accepting of others. I soon felt as if I'd known her all my life. She became the grandmother I never knew. There was no other woman in my life who was experienced and wise with age.

Therefore, not long after I began cleaning for her, I started finishing the housework in record time. We'd eat lunch together and spend the afternoon playing games. She loved checkers and cards, which neither of us seemed to tire of. Or, she'd let me brush her hair which was still black and shiny with very little gray in spite of her seventy-odd years. Afterwards we would sit on the porch swing as she told me stories of her youth and the War Between the States. She lived in Georgia then, but fled west after the war ended. Her husband died a few years later, so now she lived humbly by herself.

I stood at her doorstep knocking and waiting. It usually took her a while to get to the door so I expected to have to wait. When it opened at last, a huge grin spread over her face like the sun rising. I grabbed her hands and squeezed as we basked in each other's presence. As we stood there, I glanced down at her hands. Throughout my stay in Illinois, it was her hands I remembered most. They were thin and bony with lots of extra skin on them. The veins in her hands were dark purple and stood in contrast to her light complexion. The ends of her fingers were flattened and calloused from years of hard work. No one could call them beautiful, yet I loved them. I spent seven years holding those hands and watching them do things for me. Love flooded through me as I gazed at them now.

"Rachel, where did you come from? Are you back to stay?" Agnes looked at me with hope in her eyes, as a puppy does when it wants your attention.

"No," I shook my head. "I'm only here for a day. Fay is getting married, so we came back for a short visit."

Agnes' expression mirrored sadness for just a moment but quickly recovered and squeezed my hands tighter. "Well, it's wonderful to see you now. Can you come in and visit for a while?"

"Of course. There's no one I'd rather be with."

I'd intended to make several visits that day but couldn't bear to leave Agnes. I told her all about Fay and Arthur and shyly about Tory. She asked me lots of questions about him and made me promise to invite her to the wedding if it came to that, which made me blush with the thought.

I wanted to tell her about how I'd discovered a new relationship with God, yet I was afraid she wouldn't understand and that I'd put a wedge in our precious camaraderie. Finally, I became like the prophet Jeremiah and blurted it out because it was like fire in my bones not to. To my surprise, and yet not really, Aunt Agnes nodded in approval as I poured out my tale.

"You understand what I'm talking about, Aunt Agnes?"

"I certainly do. I made the same decision to follow Christ when I was your age. I'm afraid I haven't talked about it as much as I should have, but I've always hoped it would show in the way I lived my life." A small cloud of concern darkened her forehead. I hurried to comfort her.

"Oh, it does! Somehow I knew you would know what I was talking about. Your life reflects so much of Him." The lines in her face relaxed and we even prayed together before I left.

Fay and I both left Bevel able to close this chapter of our lives in peace. Our leaving before had been too sad. This time was full of celebration. As we headed back to Wesley, the train made a long stop in Springfield, Illinois. Fay and I walked around the station, trying to stretch our legs when I ran into Garvin Pierce. When he saw me, he put on a haughty face, trying to convince me that our last episode had not hurt his dignity. He didn't even speak to me or tip his hat. Instead he turned on his heels and began to flirt with a nearby girl, making sure I could hear every word. I whispered something unrelated to Fay who knew nothing about Garvin, but got us both laughing, which disturbed Garvin a great deal. I knew he thought we were laughing at him. In spite of it all, I couldn't help but feel sorry for him. I managed to pray for him, but wanted more than ever to get home to Tory.

15

LONELINESS

As it turned out, I didn't see Tory for a long time after we returned home. He hired himself out to help with spring planting besides working in his father's store, which kept him busy continually. It was just as well since I worked on Fay's wedding dress every spare minute, but it made me feel as though I'd wrongly assumed the security of my relationship with Tory. After all, he hadn't made any commitment to me.

Fay wired Emily and Adam in Montana as soon as she and Arthur made their announcement. I know she hoped they might come for the wedding, but a letter from our sister confirmed that this would be impossible. She sent Fay some china pieces she painted as a wedding gift and made Fay promise she would name her first daughter after her, since Emily had never been able to have children. The idea made me shudder since our oldest sister, Angela, died in childbirth, as well as my mother's trouble after I was born.

We finished the wedding dress with a full week to spare so that I had time to work on a few items for Arthur, without any tricks this time. Fay spent every minute baking. She was nervous enough about all the details for the both of us.

The day finally came. We decorated Uncle Charles' home with satin ribbons and forsythia sprigs entwined with evergreens. When Uncle Charles sat down at the piano to play, my emotions grabbed me by the throat and shook me. I felt like a rag doll that had lost all its stuffing. Somehow I hadn't faced the fact that Fay wouldn't be living with us anymore. I'd never had to manage without her, didn't even know if I could. And I was a little worried that Uncle Charles and I would become even thinner without her wonderful cooking.

Fortunately, the ceremony began, forcing my attention off myself. Everything went smoothly and all our guests distracted me for the remainder of the afternoon. However, when the day ended and everyone left, including Fay, loneliness came crashing down on me again as if a thunderstorm unleashed itself over my head. As Uncle Charles, John, and I waded through a mountain of dishes, the men tried to make light conversation but my heart wasn't in it. Uncle Charles sensed my pain and asked me if I'd like to sing some songs and pray. I shook my head, feeling guilty for refusing him, but I could no sooner sing than dance right now.

Even praying sounded hard. I thought of Jacob as he wrestled with God before he went to meet Esau. He ultimately submitted to God, but not until after the fight with Him. I was still in the fighting stage. I knew God would win, but I couldn't help struggling anyway. In fact, I wonder if anyone can understand what submission to God means without the spiritual combat.

The next day, I decided to visit the Sowders. I'd not been there for several weeks because of all the details in preparing for the wedding. Plus, I couldn't stand to stay in the house without Fay right now.

Helen was trying to keep her children cleaner and better behaved, but it often seemed a losing battle. She had so much to do and at least one child was always sick. Today there were three children crying and clinging. I took a deep breath and pitched in. At first I simply tried to do some laundry and dishes, but soon I dropped everything to take one of the children. Henry was out playing baseball, but I called him in to finish the dishes, making him angry with me. But his eyes did not narrow into slits and he obeyed.

As I patted Beth on my knee, Helen juggled the other two. When they'd calmed down, we were able to talk. "Has the doctor seen them yet, Helen?"

"No, it don't seem bad enough to call him yet."

"If they're not better tomorrow, I'll fetch him myself."

Beth particularly worried me because she was so lethargic, not at all her perky self. "Has Lars been back, Helen?"

"He was here two days ago. I'd rather he didn't come at all. I know that's a terrible thing to say about a husband, but he ne'er be much a one."

"I don't blame you a bit, Helen. Where does he go?"

"Don't know. Never bothers to tell me; just orders me around. If I ask questions, he slaps me. Ye know he was always gruff, but at least he treated me decent when we courted. He were so handsome and strong and wanted me so bad. I thought he'd settle down, not be so wild when we married, but he only got worse."

Helen rarely spoke of Lars but now she poured out her past with him. "My parents came here from Scotland when I was about six years old. We lived near Chicago until I was twelve when we moved to Wesley. I never felt I belonged here, more as if I were visiting. When I was but fourteen, I met Lars." She paused with a low moan, as if she were remembering it with fondness and with pain. "He came to see me almost everyday. My parents had no liking for him and forbade me to see him again. I ignored them and met him in private whenever I could. I was certain they just didn't understand," she added passionately, as if she were arguing the point all over again with me. "Just a year after Lars came into my life, my parents died. A tornado hit our farm, collapsing the house with them inside. I was in town working as a cook for the restaurant, so I was spared. I married Lars a week later, his child already growing within me."

I felt embarrassed that she had revealed such an intimate secret to me. I began to tell her that she shouldn't speak of such things when I remembered that the apostle James instructs us to confess our faults to one another.

The children's cries brought us back to the present duties at hand. As we tried to make them comfortable, they seemed all that mattered now. Whatever decisions had brought their troubles were of little consequence now. Better they are forgotten and we move on from here.

I went home weary at the end of the day. I would check on them again tomorrow and make sure Doc Jamison saw them. I may have suffered more over them if Henry had not slipped his hand into mine as he walked me to the buckboard. I know this seems a small display of affection but for Henry it was worth a dozen hugs and kisses.

16

ENCOUNTERING GARVIN ONCE MORE

The following day I fetched Doc Jamison because Helen's children were no better. After explaining the situation to him, he immediately left for their place. I admired Doc almost as much as Uncle Charles. He looked haggard today, but didn't complain when I told him about the Sowders. There was so much sickness this time of year; it surprised me to find him in. Helen couldn't pay him, but later told me that Uncle Charles tried to make up for it by giving Doc a little extra when he could.

Since I was in town, I stopped to see Fay. I was sure in spite of her newlywed euphoria that she must be as lonely as I was, especially with Arthur gone all day. Even if she wasn't, I could help her around the house. As I turned to climb into the buckboard, I felt a hand on my arm. "Hello, stranger."

"Tory! It's so good to see you."

"I noticed you as I was carrying a customer's purchase to his wagon. How have you been?"

"Just wonderful. My sister is married now, you know."

"I sure do. Is that why you're here, to see her?" Was there a tinge of disappointment in that question or was it just my imagination?

"Well, it's one of the reasons. Helen's children are sick so I told Doc Jamison."

"Not Henry, I hope."

"No. He's sturdy as ever."

Tory nodded his head and smiled as he thought of solid little Henry before continuing. "I'm glad I found you here. Did you know Billy Sunday is going to be holding a tent meeting in a couple of weeks? I thought we could go and take Henry."

"I've heard a lot about him. I'd like to hear him speak. What made you think of Henry?"

"Why, Billy was a baseball player."

"Of course, how perfect!"

"I thought perhaps you would come with me to church this Sunday. I know you go regularly with your uncle, but my parents would like you to attend ours and have dinner with us afterward. If it's all right, I'll pick you up at nine o'clock."

"That would be fine. I'll look forward to it."

"I've got to get back to work. See you Sunday."

I nearly flew to Fay's house, a pretty little white house with green shutters a few blocks from Main Street. I thought it rather storybook with its gingerbread peaks and rounded windows; a perfect first house. The smell of mincemeat permeated the house as I stepped through the kitchen door, bringing back the days I would pick the plump raisins out of the crock when I was small.

"How dare you make mincemeat without me around," I said as I popped through the door.

"Rachel! It's Arthur's favorite, you know. How are you?" She wiped her hands on her apron and leaned over to kiss me on the cheek.

"I miss you terribly. This married life better be worth it for me to make such a sacrifice."

Fay's smile drifted gently upward, as if smiling too quickly would ruin the moment. "It is. I can't believe I was lucky enough to find Arthur." Then she began vigorously stirring the mincemeat once more. "How's Uncle Charles?"

"Fine, but thinner already. Have you met any of the neighbors yet?"

"Yes, the Colteaux family lives two houses down. You know, they own the restaurant in town, and the Montelius family from church is right next door. She's a lovely person. I'm sure we'll be good friends. Oh, Maggie Phlox lives on this street too. She's an awful gossip. Her first greeting to me had to do with you and Garvin Pierce.

I don't know where she'd get an idea like that. I don't even know who the fellow is. I'm afraid I lost my temper with her. I'll avoid her like the plague in the future."

I laughed to myself at the thought of Maggie facing Fay's fiery temper with her eyes flashing and her finger pointed squarely at her, but I wanted to change the subject as soon as possible. It was a little alarming to know that she was spreading gossip around that actually had a basis in fact. "Oh well, I'm not worried about Maggie Phlox hurting my reputation," I lied. "By the way, you won't be seeing me on Sunday. I'm going to church with the Hampton family." I couldn't help saying it with a smack of pride.

"I think this is getting serious, Rachel," Fay teased with a sparkle in her eye. "But I'll be sure not to tell Maggie."

We laughed and hugged as I left to go back to the farm, although it seemed unnatural to leave Fay.

As I rode in the warm spring sunshine, I marveled at all that had happened in a year. I felt as if life was as good as it could be. I began to sing a hymn at the top of my lungs, not noticing the buggy that pulled up behind me. "Do you fancy yourself a singer too?" The familiar voice made my heart sink.

"Garvin Pierce. What are you doing out here?"

His eyebrows rose and chin lifted up as he replied. "Why? Is this country hallowed ground for only royalty such as you?"

"Don't be ridiculous. You were wrong and you know it." I was through dancing around the issue between this young man and me.

"Why don't you stop that wagon so we can talk without our voices jumping?"

"Can I trust you?"

"I swear on the Bible."

I sighed. It was the one thing he could have said that got my attention. I pulled on the reins until Patches stopped. "Now, what do you want to talk about?"

"You. You've ruined my reputation, you know."

"I ruined your reputation? How ludicrous."

"Why don't you like me?"

"You are no gentleman for all the airs you put on."

Suddenly Garvin's appearance changed. For the first time I saw what could be called a grave expression on his face. "I don't know. I've always thought I had all the answers. Lately everything's falling apart."

I was shocked. His arrogance left him like leaves of a maple drift to the ground in a strong breeze, leaving him naked and vulnerable.

"What happened, Garvin?" I asked in concern.

"My pop's business has gone bust. Farmers in these parts just aren't' ready for all these newfangled machines. I figure we're about five or six years ahead of the times. I'm used to doing as I please, but now I can't even afford the train passage to the next city."

"You'll find something else, Garvin. It may not be as good paying, but you'll manage."

"You don't understand. After traveling all over, sticking around someplace like Wesley will be stifling. I can't get used to such a dull life again. I need excitement. And money."

In spite of his handsome good looks, he looked a pitiful man when the flash of his life was taken away. I couldn't help but feel sorry for him. "You're living for all the wrong things, Garvin. That's why you're so miserable. I'm sorry about your father's business, but there's more to life than making money." He looked at me with blank eyes, not buying any of it. "I tell you what. Tory and I are going to hear Billy Sunday in a couple of weeks. Why don't you come with us?"

"Billy Sunday!" He brightened at the thought. "I'm no religious fellow but I heard he's pretty good; better than

George Cohen, the showman, according to the Chicago Sun Times review. That might just be a lark. I'll do it! When is it?"

"May second at two o'clock."

"I'll just come to your place about one, then. See you!" He picked up his reins and blew past me.

As soon as he moved on, I felt as if I'd just accepted a date with Attila the Hun. "This should be interesting. I've invited Garvin to accompany Tory and me. I must be crazy." I started the buckboard moving again when a new thought occurred to me. "Oh no, what is Maggie Phlox going to say about this?"

17

TRAGEDY

When I arrived home, I was surprised to find Doc Jamison there having an intense discussion with Uncle Charles. The look on his face made my heart jump into my throat. "What's wrong, Doc?"

"I've just come from the Sowders, Rachel. You know little Beth has been sick much longer than the other two children."

"No, I didn't know."

"According to Helen, she's had this flu for two weeks. She should've seen me earlier, but Helen thought it would pass." As Doc spoke I had a sinking feeling in my stomach, almost wishing he wouldn't go on. "I believe the older children do have a common flu, but I'm afraid Beth may have polio."

"Oh no!" I tried to keep the tears from coming but they steamed down my face in spite of my efforts. Uncle Charles put an arm around me and held me close.

"It may not have lasting results for her. It's too soon to tell. Sometimes the disease is mild and passes without causing any permanent damage. Beth is having trouble standing which worries me a great deal. She's only been walking a few months, which makes it hard to tell whether she is weak from the sickness or if it is affecting her muscles.

"Rachel, I would like you to take some personal responsibility for her. Visit her at least every other day. If you notice any trouble in her breathing, swallowing, or eye movement, fetch me immediately. Can you do that?"

Being given something to do about the situation gave me new courage. I dried my eyes and straightened my shoulders. "Of course I can. I'll write down those things, so I'll remember what to look for." Doc smiled in approval. "Is Helen all right, Doc?"

Doc's face drooped, looking like a sail that lies crumbled when the wind dies down. "She was numb when I told her. I worry that the strain of this might cause her to break. That's why you are of such importance. She can't face this alone."

After Doc left, I went to my room, now absent of Fay's things, and threw myself on the bed praying passionately for Beth. I asked God to heal her and begged for an answer to why she had to suffer so. In my need, I flipped through my Bible, looking for answers. I turned to the book of Romans as I had been reading there of late. My eyes fell on the first verse of the fifteenth chapter, "We then that are strong ought to bear the infirmities of the weak, and not to please ourselves." This was the only answer I had from God right now. He'd let me know more as I obeyed this command. I didn't need to know all of His reasons. I needed to trust Him in Beth's life and do what I could to help her. I fulfilled my promise to Doc Jamison over the next two weeks. I went every other day, spending a great deal of time just rocking and watching Beth. Her vomiting and fever were gone now but it was all too clear that the muscles in her legs had been affected. At first she was in such great pain, that she screamed when we tried to help her stand. Helen couldn't bear to hear her baby in such distress, so I began to send her outside with the others as I worked with Beth. After the second week, it was worse. Beth no longer screamed as I placed her on her feet; she simply crumpled to the floor.

When I returned home that awful day, I reported to John and Uncle Charles the terrible news. John, whose attitude had slowly changed toward the Sowders family, was the first to speak.

"As I sees it, the problim is gonna be Miss Helen's tryin' ta cart that baby aroun'. She needs a wheel chair of sorts. I'll git on that right away if you don't mind, Mista Bradbury."

"You take all the time you need, John. The fields are ready for planting, but we can wait a few days." I think Uncle

Charles would have sacrificed his crop for the year to see John complete this project.

John's hands flew as he worked on the chair, which he finished in three days. I made a leather cushion for the seat and back of the tiny wheelchair. More accurately, it was a buggy with a seat on it. John's cousin gave him a baby buggy that was worn beyond use on the top but in good repair on the base. It would be a comfortable ride for Beth.

John decided to deliver the chair himself, his first volunteer visit to the Sowders family. He'd been there on errands for Uncle Charles, but never out of his own concern for them.

It pleased him a great deal to put Beth in it. Henry instantly offered to give her a ride. After whirling around the small house a few times as fast as he could go, he had Beth giggling, the first smile we'd seen since her sickness began. We soon graduated him to the great outdoors with many warnings as to the value of his precious cargo. By the time we left, the color returned to Beth's cheeks.

Although small progress, it encouraged us nonetheless. If her brothers and sister could accept her, it would have a great deal to do with whether she would accept her lot in life. Although that would be easy now, it would become more difficult the older she grew. Surely her siblings would become better people as they learned to have compassion on their sister. It was too early to tell if Beth would be a fighter or if she would succumb to her circumstances. I began to pray that she would be tough.

At any rate, this day was a turning point. We were doing something to make the situation tolerable. Beth, in her helplessness, brought out the love in all of us.

18

BILLY SUNDAY

During these stressful weeks, I attended church with Tory, my emotional and spiritual life renewed in his presence in this place. Tory's rich, full tenor voice comforted me as he sang with gusto.

A day spent in the Hampton home was delightful. Gone were my fears of his parents as they welcomed me as one of their own. Mrs. Hampton particularly showed interest in Beth Sowders and began crocheting a sweater and lap blanket for me to take to her.

It wasn't until our trip back to the farm that I told Tory that Garvin would be accompanying us to hear Billy Sunday.

"You invited Garvin to go along with us?" Tory's voice raised an octave with each word. I can't even describe the way he said Garvin's name.

"Who could need to hear Billy Sunday more than Garvin? I thought it would be really good for him." I tried to keep my voice light and cheerful.

"Have you forgotten what he's like? The way he treated you on the bridge? I can't believe you'd even be seen with him?"

"I know. It's just that he stopped me to talk and Billy Sunday came up. It seemed the right thing to do at the time."

"Well, it's not the right thing to do. You'll just have to uninvite him."

I stared at Tory as if he'd just told me to run the rest of the way home. "I can't do that. It would be so rude. Besides, I'm glad he's coming. I think he needs to go."

Tory turned to the front, almost trembling with anger. Finally he said in a voice that was so quiet that I had to lean closer to hear him. "Maybe the two of you should just go without me."

Now I was mad. "Don't be ridiculous. I can't go alone with Garvin. That would look terrible."

"Well, everyone will know I didn't invite him." We were both yelling now. I was mad enough to spit. If I could have run all the way home, I would have. As soon as I saw the farm, I took the reins from Tory's hands and yanked back on them, stopping his team. I stepped down without any assistance from him. "I'll see you as we planned. Garvin is coming, so you'll just have to make the best of it. As a man of your word, I know you'll come." I then walked towards the house as quickly as my full skirts would take me. Tory turned the team around in record time and rode away at a brisk trot.

As soon as I got inside, I felt miserable about my behavior. Why couldn't I have been reasonable, instead of so snippy? I wished I could talk to Tory again to take back some of the harshness of my words, but it was too late.

Garvin arrived before Tory on the day we were to go. For a moment, I had the terrifying thought that maybe Tory wouldn't come and I'd have to go with him by myself. I'd hoped that Tory would come first so that we could talk about it, but that was not to be. To make things even worse, Garvin was back to his haughty self. "Well, Rachel, you look beautiful as always. Think this Sunday fellow will live up to his reputation? I'm looking forward to a good show."

"It's more than a show, Garvin; it's a message to which you would do well to listen carefully." I knew there was a little too much spite in my voice. Why did I find it so hard to talk civilly to this man?"

"Nah. I'm just going for the show. I told you I was no religious man." I felt a sort of hopelessness when he said this. I'd jeopardized my relationship with Tory for the likes of this fellow? I decided it would be best to change the subject.

"Do you have a job yet, Garvin?"

"No, I'm living off a trust fund my pop set up for me. It's great. I have plenty of time to do as I please and plenty of money to do it with."

"What happens when it's gone?"

"Oh, Pop will have a new income by then, which I'll be glad to help him spend." His chuckle was like chalk screeching on slate. I bit my tongue because I knew if I said anything, my hot temper would flare.

Tory pulled up in his buggy before I had to endure Garvin's comments any longer. I smiled at him but he looked straight ahead as if neither of us were there. Fortunately, there was only room for two in the front, so Garvin had to sit in the back. Henry wanted to sit with Tory and me so he squeezed between us when we arrived to pick him up.

Tory never said more than a greeting to any of us. I could see that Henry was visibly hurt that Tory didn't have a peppermint for him. It would have been a very silent trip if Garvin had not spoken his nonsense all the way. How could a person talk so much about nothing?

As we pulled up to the tent, I was astounded at all the people there. I'd seen this many people gathered at fairs before, but never for any other event. In spite of the sober mood we arrived in, the excitement in the air began to affect us all. Garvin began talking twice as fast.

"This reminds me of the farm machinery conventions in Chicago. Of course, they covered a larger area than this..." I noticed Tory rolling his eyes as he put up with Garvin's chatter. It was then that I began to pray that Tory's patience would hold up. I began to be slightly afraid that Garvin might get a bloodied nose.

Henry surprised me most. Generally so sober, he almost skipped. All at once he turned to Garvin, "Why don' you just shud-up." Tory broke into a roar of laughter as he swooped down to pick up Henry in a bear hug. I was so shocked, I couldn't even scold Henry. Garvin was miffed, but he did shut up.

Soon everyone gathered on the benches waiting anxiously for Billy to appear. There was a buzz of conversation, yet an air of expectation. Everyone kept their eyes toward the platform, even as they talked to their neighbor. Before long, a song leader appeared. As I think back on this day, this was my favorite part. That great group of people singing the new hymn, *To God Be the Glory,* sounded like the multitudes of heaven. I know nothing that has convinced me more of my privileges in Christ than singing with all those people. All the times I felt alone in my pilgrimage with the Lord melted away in this experience. I determined to remember it when I was once more alone in my day-to-day activities.

The congregation now burst with enthusiasm. When Billy Sunday stepped to the platform, there was a great round of applause, then such a hush one could hear a pin drop.

Small in stature, his booming voice made up for his size.
Exaggerated motions accompanied his words, making it
easy to keep everyone's attention. His baseball moves
came out with every word. I'd been worried about Henry
sitting still for the message, but now I saw that this had
been a fruitless concern. Unlike the staid ministers we
were all used to, this man reminded me of the ringmaster
at a circus I'd been to once. I relaxed immediately until I
caught a glimpse of Garvin. His arms were folded over his
chest, his chin high and a smirk of disdain on his face. In
contrast to those around him, he looked like a lion about
to pounce on his prey. I started wondering just why he
came.

Billy used many baseball illustrations throughout his
speech. He had the gift of causing us all to laugh, then
hitting us with some profound and serious truth which
sank all the deeper in contrast to the light moments.

As he closed his sermon with a challenge for all to "get
right with God", many rose to go to the front of the tent
to shake Billy's hand, a sign of their commitment to follow
Christ. Out of the corner of my eye, I saw a movement, so
I turned to see if perhaps Henry wanted to go forward.
Instead, I was shocked to see Garvin move out into the
aisle and start forward. Tory looked at me with his eyes
wide and his mouth ajar, reminding me of baby Beth
when someone makes a loud noise. Even more
astonishing, Garvin's shoulders shook with sobs as he
reached for Billy's hand, so that Billy pulled him into an
embrace. I couldn't help but feel a quiver of excitement

run through me at the sight, but I remained a bit skeptical too. I wondered if Garvin's display of emotion would stick.

When it was all over, Garvin walked slowly back to us. "I apologize, Rachel, for treating you badly that night on the bridge. I knew it was wrong then, but couldn't admit it to myself. I've been wrong for so long, that I didn't know how to get out of it."

Then he turned to Tory, who still looked wide-eyed. "Tory, forgive me for the many times I made fun of you in our school days. It was only because I was jealous of your calm spirit and kind heart. I wanted to be like you but didn't know how to do it. These thoughts have been coming to me for a while, but I didn't know how to face them until today. What Billy said about Jesus Christ making us new creatures gives me hope." He then climbed into the carriage and leaned his head on his hands.

Tory and I hesitantly climbed in also, looking at each other the way kittens that have just opened their eyes look at their mother. Henry sat in the back with Garvin this time, staring at him as if he'd just found his best friend. I finally found my voice, "What did Billy say that struck you so, Garvin?"

"All of it. While everyone else laughed, I tried to smile. It was easy at first, but the more he spoke, the more uncomfortable I got. You see, his stories were all about me. I was the person in every one of them. The shame of my life was a laughing matter to everyone else. But when he spoke of Christ's forgiveness for me, it tore all the past away and gave me a future. One where I could be a person I respected and that others would too. I want this more than I've ever wanted anything."

Tory now turned around to face him. "That's great, Garvin. I'm sorry I never thought of talking to you about these things, instead of ignoring you. I'm ashamed of myself. But I'd love to be a part of this new beginning for you. I have as much to learn as you do. Maybe we can work on this together."

"Thank you, Tory. That would be a great privilege and an honor."

We rode in silence the rest of the way home, all of us stunned by what had just happened. When we arrived at Henry's house, I walked him to the door. "What did you think of the meeting, Henry?"

He looked at me with the intensity of his narrowed eyes that reminded me of the first encounter I'd had with him. "I'm gonna grow up to do what Billy Sunday does - help people like Mista Pierce."

As Henry disappeared into the house and I settled back into the buggy, Tory leaned over to me speaking softly, "I've never seen anything like this. It beats all. Since apologies seem in order today, I offer you mine too." My heart warmed as if Pocahontas had built a fire in it.

19

JAIL!

I slept later than usual the next morning because the rain drizzling down the windows hid the sun and provided a soothing noise that drowned out the normal hustle and bustle of the farm. What began as a gentle rain soon turned into a classic spring storm with thunder clashing and wind roaring. I've always loved storms. I love the display of power and the contrasting feeling of being safe and cozy inside. It was also a perfect excuse to curl up with a book and ignore some of the more pressing activities facing my day, something Fay would have scolded me for, but that I had perfect freedom to do now.

That's how I found myself curled on the horsehide sofa engrossed in another world. I always enter the world I'm reading about, oblivious to others going about their way in our every day life. Through books I explore far reaches of the world, fall in love a hundred times, try any profession, follow any dream. I have the privilege of knowing great minds, being challenged by those whose world is different than mine and comforted by those who are the same.

While living in this other place, I became aware of someone rustling around in the dining room. I have no idea how long this person had been there, but decided to investigate since Uncle Charles had a meeting in town and John usually didn't come in without knocking. I wondered if Uncle Charles had returned, but I couldn't imagine it in this storm. In fact, I worried that he might not get back at all unless it let up.

As I entered the dining room, I gave a shriek and dropped my book. A large, dark man, dripping wet from head to toe stood hunched over Uncle Charles' silverware case, stuffing cutlery into a bag. At my scream he looked up and turned towards me. As he narrowed his eyes, I sucked in my breath in recognition of Lars Sowders.

"One word of this and I'll kill you, hear me?" he said in that agonizingly low voice as he advanced slowly toward me. The words caught in my throat as I finally forced them out. "Why didn't you tell my uncle you needed help? He would gladly have provided employment for you."

Lars broke into a laugh that sounded like a witches cackle as he swore at me. "You think I'd ever ask that meddlin' uncle of yours fo anythin'? I get what I need my own way. Shut up about this or you'll never talk again 'bout nothin'." He started to go but then thought better of it. "I hear you've taken a likin' to my Henry. If this gets out, he'll pay along with you." He then fled out the door, leaving it wide open.

I shuddered as I pushed the door shut, locating the skeleton key on the windowsill and turning it quickly, before Lars changed his mind and came back. I went around to the back door and locked it with the same key. Then I checked every window on the first floor, locking them tightly. After that I even went upstairs and locked all of those, but I didn't want to stay upstairs. I wanted to be downstairs, alert and waiting. I sat down at the kitchen table, confused and frightened.

Poor Helen. What a horrible thing to be married to that man. I asked God to protect her and the children, driving some of the fear for myself away. I was still rather amazed that Lars hadn't hurt me. Perhaps he hadn't slid that far yet, but I it seemed a fine line to step over at this point.

I thought of going out to find, John, but I was afraid to step outside of the house for fear Lars still lurked out there somewhere. A verse from the fourth chapter of the book of Philippians kept running through my mind. "...whatsoever things are true, whatsoever things are honest, whatsoever things are just, whatsoever things are pure, whatsoever things are lovely, whatsoever things are of good report, if there be any virtue, and if there be any praise, think on these things." Fixing my mind on the One who was in control of even this situation brought me a peace that was not natural.

Time went slowly that day. When the storm let up and Uncle Charles came home, I sighed in relief, like a lost lamb who has just made it back to the security of the flock. He was surprised that I'd locked the door, so I answered it as soon as he banged on it, making me jump with the tension of it. Letting him in, I related the events of the day. "What are we going to do, Uncle Charles?"

"I don't know, Rachel. This will take some thought. I've always wondered what Lars lived on. I've heard of other thefts around these parts, fearing Lars could be involved. He's a violent man. I'm just thankful you weren't hurt."

"He certainly wants me to think he will hurt me if I report his crime. I'm most worried about Helen and the children. He takes everything out on them."

"We'll check on them first thing in the morning. For now, let's eat supper. I'm famished."

I went to bed early that night, anxious for this day to be over. The next morning dawned bright, all trace of the storm gone, the warm rays of the sun prying my eyes open from their long rest. When I found Uncle Charles in the kitchen, he looked as though he'd slept little. "We cannot let Lars control everyone by his threats. We'll have to tell Sheriff Miller right away. Will you be willing to testify in court against him?"

I trembled at the thought of having to face him again. Part of me hoped he'd just go away and never return again. I bowed my head for a moment, but when I looked up I knew what my answer had to be. "Of course, but what about Helen and the children?"

"We'll bring them here until Lars is apprehended. I'll leave now to get them. I'll send John into town on Patches to tell the sheriff. Lady can pull the buckboard alone today."

I nodded, feeling frightened at the prospect of being alone on the farm again. "Do you want me to go with you?"

"No, why don't you get things ready for the Sowders family. We'll need some clean sheets and blankets for everyone."

The next few days were excruciating. Helen looked like a beaten donkey, as if there were no hope for her life. Henry noticed this and took it on himself, ignoring the other children's games and staring out the window. Beth became his only distraction as he pushed her around in her chair. I tried talking to Henry about what happened, but he refused to speak of it, torn between his love for his mother and his fear of his father.

Word finally came on the third day that Lars had been apprehended. We all sighed with relief. The trial was to take place in Paxton, the county seat, which is where Lars was being held in the county jail.

Over the course of the last three days, Uncle Charles, Helen, and I prayed for Lars and asked God for wisdom in how to handle the situation once he was incarcerated.

We were reluctant to see him go to jail. None of us wanted that, so we agreed that Uncle Charles would see him and offer to drop all charges if he would make restitution to everyone he'd stolen from. If anyone else wanted to press charges, Uncle Charles would do his best to make peace with them. We all agreed it was worth a try.

So upon hearing of Lars' arrest, Uncle Charles left to see him. When he returned, he wore a long face. I saw Helen's expression of expectancy turn to disappointment. We'd all hoped beyond hope that if Lars had to face prison, that he'd be willing to change his ways.

As Uncle Charles settled into his easy chair, he let out a big sigh, "What a frustrating conversation. Lars refused to listen to me at all until he heard me say something about a way out for him. However, after disclosing our solution, he rejected it. Evidently he felt others would have no mercy. I guess he has little regard for my influence over them. He also couldn't pay; over half the things he'd stolen were gone. He traded them to an outside man who paid him with money long since spent."

When Uncle Charles finished, Helen, who'd been seated, rose slowly and walked out of the room. I could see that her eyes were wet with tears. I followed her but found her on her knees in anguish and petition. Rather than interrupt her I knelt beside her, adding prayers of my own. After all, only God could meet the deepest needs of her heart and soul now. Nothing I could say would really help.

Uncle Charles told me later, "I made the story of my encounter with Lars milder for Helen's sake. He's a bitter man. More foul language came out of his mouth than I've ever heard before, and he interrupted me continually. If the guards hadn't been there, I'm sure he would have attacked me. He also has no regret for any of his crimes. In fact, he said his only regret was leaving you alive that day. The man chills me to the bone. Perhaps if I'd paid more attention to him in the past…" Uncle Charles' voice trailed off into a tone of regret.

"You've done everything God put in your heart to do, Uncle Charles. Don't let Lars destroy your peace of mind."

He took my hands gratefully and squeezed them. "There's nothing to do now but wait for the trial."

20

THE TRIAL

Tory visited us as soon as he heard the news. His concern melted all the animosity that was left between us after the incident with Garvin. His affect on Henry was wonderful as he involved him in a game of baseball and brought peppermints for all the children. After supper he treated us all to some music on his mandolin as we sang along to *In The Good Ol' Summertime* and *Take Me Home Again, Kathleen*.

When the evening ended, I walked Tory to his carriage. "Thank you for bringing us so much cheer. It was just what we all needed. I even saw Helen smile."

Tory acknowledged my thanks but I could see that he was agitated. "Are you sure you should testify at that trial, Rachel?"

If I could see my own face, I'm sure my mouth was in a line and my eyes wide. "I wish there was some way I could get out of it. If it had only been us that he robbed, I think I would be tempted to drop it, but he also robbed old Mrs. Alder in town a few weeks before he robbed us. She caught him as I did but didn't say anything because he threatened her. She was brave enough to come forward when she heard that he was apprehended. Poor woman, she must have been terrified living all alone." I paused and looked out into the distance. "I've never been so frightened in my life; not killing water moccasins, not seeing my father die, nothing compares to this. I've had trouble sleeping at night since it happened. I'm constantly hearing noises and seeing shadows, even though I know he's in custody."

"That's just it. Why not just end it. I don't want to see you tangled up in this anymore."

I nodded. "But the alternative is that someone else has to do it. No, it's up to me, Tory. I need you to help me be strong enough, not try to talk me out of it."

He picked up my hands in his, looking me in the eyes. "I'll try, but if I end up kidnapping you and taking you away, don't be surprised." Then a slow smile lit up his face, like the sun rising over the prairie, sending a thrill from my toes to my nose. I liked this man so much, it hurt. And it was really hard not to tell him to go ahead and kidnap me right now.

"I wish I could do it for you, Rachel," he added in a soft voice as the smile left and his brows furrowed like the fields that surrounded us. All of a sudden, I'd had enough of this serious talk. If he persisted, I'd grab him and kiss him right there and then, which would have shocked poor

Fay to the core, so instead I pushed him away playfully and laughed, "I do too!"

I broke the spell out of necessity for both our sakes, and Tory left with a smile on his face.

The weeks dragged on as we awaited the trial. When the day finally came, Fay watched Helen's children so the three of us could make the trip to Paxton. As we entered the courtroom, Helen began to tremble. "I can't do this, Rachel. I can't be here to watch Lars be sentenced to prison."

I sat down with her and hugged her. "If you need to leave any time during the proceeding, go ahead. We will all understand." She began to calm down as I held her hand, but her face looked like she had the pox, it was so red and blotchy. How I wish I could comfort her instead of pointing a finger at her husband.

"What will it be like for my children, Rachel, to have to face everyone in town when they all know about their father?"

"I don't know, Helen. We just have to take a day at a time and trust God with the details. Today you just have to get through this trial."

Helen took courage in these words and straightened her shoulders as she turned to me. "I know it's crazy, but in

Gathering Bittersweet

spite of all that's happened, I still love Lars. I still want him to change and be a father to his children. I want to believe that could happen."

I had no words for that. I just took her hand in mine and squeezed it tightly. At that moment Lars appeared, causing Helen's hand to take a death grip on mine. He looked awful. His hair hadn't been washed or combed for week. His beard was scruffy and ragged, looking as if a host of creatures lived inside of it. His clothes were clean, probably courtesy of the jail, but they were worn and ragged. His eyes had dark circles underneath, almost as if someone had rubbed coal dust underneath them, but they held the same narrow gaze of contempt. I thought of his dependence on liquor and how ragged he must feel now without it to numb his senses. He never looked at Helen, which perhaps was best.

The trial went quickly. Lars made no defense for himself so my testimony stood unopposed. The prosecuting attorney had recovered some of the stolen goods, so there was little doubt in the juror's minds as to the verdict. They deliberated only twenty minutes before pronouncing Lars guilty. I cried when the judge gave him three years in prison. It's a terrible thing to be the one who is responsible for sending a person to prison. This was the most agonizing thing I'd ever done. It's like spanking a disobedient child. Whenever I've done it, I feel dreadful at the time even though I know it's necessary.

During the trial Lars remained unrepentant. He showed nothing but contempt for me and burned a thousand holes in me with his eyes. In some weird twist, that made me want to visit him in jail to show God's love to him any way I could.

I wondered what could be in Lars' mind. How could he come to this point in his life and not see his great need? Could it be that he was so angry that it drove every other emotion from his mind? Or had he chosen to compare himself to those worse still, thus justifying his crimes? We all do that, in a way.

Our trip back to Wesley was silent. Helen seemed more composed now that the deed was done, or perhaps she was gaining strength to face her children. Uncle Charles and I offered to keep her little ones for a day or two, but she refused, insisting she needed them now more than ever. We would take care of her in other ways by helping her put in a big garden, and supplying meat from Uncle Charles' stock farm. I'd make clothes for the children out of extra fabric I had so they at least would have food and clothing. We wouldn't have to worry about shoes until winter.

When we reached Fay's to pick up the children, Henry came out first without a word. His expression made it clear that he knew exactly what had happened.

As Uncle Charles loaded everyone into the buckboard for the trip home, I thanked Fay for watching the children. In spite of our serious countenances, her eyes were dancing and her foot was tapping, as if a melody were playing sprightly in her mind. As I turned to go, she grabbed my arm and pulled me aside. "Rachel, I can't wait any longer to tell you the news." Now her smile tugged her mouth upward like a flag being raised on a pole. "I'm going to have a baby!"

"Really," I said hesitantly as the news sank into my bones, the way a glass of water soaks into cracked dry clay. As the truth dawned, I almost yelled, "I'm going to be an aunt!" Life does go on.

21

SWEET SUMMER

Maggie Phlox was at her old tricks, making life miserable for Fay and me. She gave Fay no peace about the fact that I'd visited Lars Sowders in jail. Actually, Fay agreed with her but defended me against Maggie's stinging arrows the way a warrior defends his tribe. There is nothing like opposition to get someone on your side.

When I saw Lars, I expressed my sorrow at having to testify against him. When he spit at me and threw the Bible I handed him into the corner, I startled like a Mexican jumping bean. I'm not sure what I thought would happen, but of course I hoped for better than this. I vacillated between sorrow and anger when I replayed the scene over and over in my mind, like Hamlet's father's death played in his.

I watched the children several times throughout the next year while Helen visited Lars, but he never had a kind word for her. The hope she once felt for him began to die like a lone ember on a cold winter night. I noticed the relief in her eyes and demeanor at the knowledge that he was locked away from her and the children, but I also

knew that fear gripped her, as it did me, at the thought of
his release.

We welcomed summer with open arms as a long lost
relative who finally comes to visit. With baseball games
back in swing, Henry was made the official water boy, the
youngest the team had ever had and the most loyal. I was
still amazed that in spite of his father's reputation, most
of the citizens of Wesley treated Henry with high regard.
No one could help but admire his hard work and
dedication to the team, giving him notoriety among the
baseball players that spread to the townsfolk. Most of
them, that is.

Tory began working his aunt's farm full time, which she
left him in her will. He made a successful start in the hog
business with Poland-China hogs, which took most of his
time. Our snatches together were few and far between
but always left me with hope that we had a future
together even though nothing had been spoken.

As for Garvin Pierce, he truly was a changed man. He got
a job as a bank teller and was very good at it, winning the
trust of the town through his friendly greetings and ready
wit. He still had a cocky air about him, but it was under
control now so that it attracted rather than repelled.
Everyone noticed the change, not the least of which was
his parents. He no longer squandered their money and
even went out of his way to be kind to them. Although his

tongue still rattled on like a dried gourd full of seeds, he now had better thoughts so his words were more worthwhile to listen to. He talked openly of how Christ had changed his life and made him a new person. Tory even began to develop a liking for the fellow.

Arthur and Fay looked like two lovebirds feathering their nest. The heat of the summer was hard on Fay since she was with child, but she was more cheerful than I'd ever seen her, even developing her sense of humor more. I particularly enjoyed one visit with her. "Well, Fay, do you think it's going to be a boy or a girl?"

"I don't know. If it's a boy, I have to name him Arthur and if it's a girl, Emily. I always thought it would be fun to try to think of a name for my child, but now it's already settled." Fay smiled like a raccoon that had just caught a fat fish, then broke into a giggle. "You wouldn't remember this, but once when Emily wanted to go to town, the horses were in the field and there was only an old mule left to pull the buggy. She was dressed in her finest, although I've forgotten why now. She always did dress with such flair! Anyway, part way there the mule got interested in a cow meandering along the road and wouldn't budge. Wherever the cow went, the mule followed. They ended up in the middle of a field and stayed there. Emily finally gave up and walked home. I still remember the look on her face!"

I joined her in the memories. "My funniest thoughts of Emily were the taffy pulls she loved. That's still my favorite treat, you know. Why don't we do that anymore?" Fay just smiled. "Well, this was at Christmas and she wanted to surprise Adam with a batch of taffy. However, when we started pulling it, she realized she'd left the pan on the stove and it started to smoke. She tried to knock it off with her elbow because we were all stuck up with taffy. Somehow she got off balance and ended up with taffy all over the place. That was the silliest sight I've ever beheld."

We continued to laugh and swap stories until the day grew late. I hated leaving Fay. I missed her more than I could have imagined.

Of course, I spent a lot of time with Helen and the children. Howard wanted Henry and me to help him do some taxidermy. He'd seen a deer in the window of the supply store in town and decided that was for him. The only trouble was that all he ever managed to trap were rats. Now I detest rats and the last thing in the world I wanted to do was immortalize one by stuffing it, but Howard's eyes were so pleading that I did my best. Henry was the one who cleaned it because I couldn't stand it. We finally stuffed the ugly thing with sawdust and Howard was as proud as if it'd been a bear. The next time I came to their home, he had three more rats waiting for me. I refused to stuff any more of the creatures; instead I talked Howard into using their skins for something else, although I couldn't think of a thing to do with a rat skin.

I'd not counted on the creativity of young minds. We spent the summer making rat fur wallets and purses, even rat fur hats, but the one that struck me the funniest was a rat fur muff for their little sister Elma. She used it all through the hot summer as proudly as if it had been rabbit's fur. I secretly hoped no one would know I'd made it. I couldn't imagine that it would do much for my sewing business.

Sometimes these summer days seemed perfect as if the winter would never come again.

22

THE MISSIONARY

New Zealand, twelve hundred miles off the coast of Australia. Just naming the place brought images of exotic scenes that pranced across my mind like a troop of show horses. I'd never known anyone out of Missouri and Illinois, so to meet a missionary who'd actually been to New Zealand excited me to my very bones.

The Squires were on furlough. Since I'm new to the church, I had to ask Uncle Charles what that meant. Evidently they were home for a year to see family, get refreshed, and raise funds to go back again. They stayed at the parson's home and shared with our congregation what their mission consisted of. I hung on every word. So when Dorothy Squire asked for someone in the congregation to help her make some clothing to take back to the Maori people of New Zealand, I jumped at the chance. Since they had a seven-year-old boy, I decided to take Henry with me as I helped.

We met at the church, where Dorothy welcomed me with open arms. "Thank you so much for coming and bringing

Henry. Our Peter has been very lonely this summer. He's used to having a whole village full of boys to play with."

I'd worried a little that Henry wouldn't meet their approval, but I soon realized that they were used to a completely different society than we were. Henry and Peter hit it off immediately. They headed outside and we hardly saw them after that.

Dorothy and I settled into each other's personalities just about as easily, reminding me of my own childhood friends, who felt like a well-worn slipper that fit perfectly to your foot. She looked to be in her late thirties or early forties, although she could have been younger. My first impression of her was that she had hard features, but after talking to her for a few minutes, I changed my mind, deciding they were strong, not hard. Forthright and honest, she spoke her mind directly, never beating around the bush. Her voice was deep and mellow; it reminded me of the roar of a contented lion I'd seen in a circus once, not harsh but full of strength. She took control of the conversation at once while we worked.

"Reverend Brown told me about the way you and your uncle have been helping the Sowders family. This is what life is all about. It's good to see a young person who understands that."

"Thank you." I felt embarrassed, yet somehow encouraged to go on. "It's been everyone together who's

helped the Sowders. I must admit Henry has become my
favorite. I try to take him with me as often as possible."

"Ah, children are one of God's most precious gifts to us."
As she spoke, she stared out the window for a moment,
looking up from the stitches we diligently placed in the
fabric in our laps, reminding me of a bee searching for
nectar. "We had to wait a long time for Peter. He's
brought more joy to our lives in seven years than I
thought possible." Her lips began to tremble, but then she
looked at me squarely, composed once again. "Of course,
it's as if we have hundreds of children in our village. They
are like our own."

"What's the name of your village?"

"Waikari. It's in the southern island of New Zealand."

"What's it like there?" With the name, I pictured a tropical
island with palms and sea grasses, like in a novel I'd read
about Florida.

"It's very mountainous where we are. There are several
volcanoes and hot springs, but also green pastures. It
rarely gets cold and the seasons are reversed. December
is one of our warmest months. Believe it or not, one of
my hardest adjustments at first was celebrating Christmas
in the summer."

"How long have you been there?"

"We went fifteen years ago with another couple. English they were, from the Cotswolds. We're the only Americans on the island to this day. There were very few English in New Zealand then, only Maori. Now the English come all the time. They raise cattle and sheep and grow wheat. It's a time of change for all of us."

"Have many Maori believed?"

"Yes, many. They are a fine people. I respect them very much. Many families are raising their children in the church. We've planted three other churches among neighboring villages since we've been there."

"What made you decide to go to New Zealand in the first place?"

"I went there...," she began, then stopped as if reconsidering. "I went because of Samuel. I must admit I never would have done it on my own. I loved God and wanted to obey Him, but this was Samuel's dream, not mine. The first year, I thought I'd die. I was lonely for family and friends and I struggled with the language something awful. I wanted to come home and told Samuel so."

"What changed your mind?"

"It was Christmas that first year. I wanted to surprise Samuel with a rug for our home. We had very few things of beauty and I missed the luxuries we'd left behind." She paused and looked as if she were pulling up feelings long gone, as a fisherman drags up an old boot when he's expecting a fish. "Anyway, I'd almost finished the rug, when I found it missing from its usual spot. As I searched for it, I found the Maori children had rolled it out on the grass. It had rained the night before, so it was muddy as could be. When I found the little girl who'd taken it, I was so angry that I shook her until her teeth rattled. She must have only been five years of age. The Maori have no experience with things like rugs, so she probably thought it was a pretty mat. As the tears streamed down her cheeks in shock and bewilderment, I grabbed the rug and toted it home.

"When I arrived back home with my bedraggled rug, I began to cry myself. At first I was just upset about the rug, but soon the pain in my heart was for that little girl. It occurred to me that this rug would last, at the most, a few years, but God whispered in my heart that this precious child would last all of eternity. I searched until I found her and began a lasting relationship with her and her family. She's now a grown woman with a young baby of her own. They're one of the most faithful families in our church."

Dorothy fell quiet as she carefully applied each stitch. I sat silently, moved by this story and unsure what to say next. I felt like a child who had wandered in on a holy man saying his prayers, embarrassed and a little bit in awe. Presently Dorothy spoke again, "So, you see, that was a turning point. I understood ever after that my life didn't consist of things to make me comfortable, but that it was to be given away to others. Samuel already knew that. It took me a while to figure it out. And do you know? Happiness followed like a feather falling to the ground on light wind." Dorothy now smiled, transforming her strong face into gentle lines of merriment.

On the way home, I asked Henry how he enjoyed his new playmate. "He's great! Did ya know he's lived his whole life haf-way 'round the world? He's been sailin' on a big ship and everythin'. Some folks got all the luck!" I grinned as I thought of how Henry's perception of missionary life was different from our adult point of view, and felt the contagion of it.

I spent as much time as I could with Dorothy until she had to leave for New Zealand. The day they left, Henry and I both mourned their absence as if someone had died. We promised to write, but knew it would take half a year for them to get the letter. I could hardly stand it. Never had I known anyone who had affected me more profoundly.

23

A LOST DAY

I had a chance to apply what I learned from Dorothy
Squire sooner than I would have liked. Fall made me feel
like I was on a runaway train. If I stayed on, I'd crash and
if I jumped, I'd get all bruised; neither option particularly
appealing. Before I could blink twice, I ran out of sewing
notions and canning supplies, making it necessary to take
a trip into town to replenish my meager stores. The
scenery flashing around me in its autumn splendor
became a blur of color. I didn't notice any of it on this
jaunt. All that was in my mind was to purchase the things
I needed and return home as quickly as possible.

It's amazing how one can treasure a lesson in one's heart
and yet miss an opportunity to use what has been
learned. I went directly to the general store which Mr.
Hampton owned. Tory no longer worked there as his
farming took all his time. Mr. Hampton himself rarely
worked there either, as he had several business ventures.
He came in and out to check on things but paid another
man, Joseph Spencer, to tend the store.

"Hello, Mr. Spencer. I need several items today. I've listed them out so if you would collect them for me, I'd be grateful." I knew my voice was abrupt and business like, but I was in a hurry. The list of things I still had to do at home could fill a newspaper. Mr. Spencer was a nice enough man, but he seemed slower than a box turtle making his way across the road today. I cleared my throat and tapped my foot, hoping he'd take the hint that he needed to hurry it up. I was about to suggest such a thing, when Mr. Hampton's strong voice rang through the air.

"Rachel, what a pleasure to see you. We've missed you at Sunday dinners lately."

"Good day to you, Sir. I've missed you too. It's just been so busy." I spoke my mind quickly, hoping this interchange would be short.

"I'm glad I've run into you. Mrs. Hampton and I have been thinking about little Beth Sowders. We would very much like to do something for her."

"That's very kind, Mr. Hampton, but I don't think there is much that can be done." I said this as if I were God himself pronouncing a judgment.

"But there is. We've been checking into it. A close friend of ours works in a school in Chicago. He works with the blind but has informed us that there's also advancement being made in helping the lame. Now, you told us Beth still has some movement in her legs. Is this correct?" I could see Mr. Hampton's face glowing with excitement which I couldn't share in the least.

"Yes, it is, but she's so weak that it does her little good."

"According to our physician friend, if enough muscles are unaffected by the polio, they can be trained to carry the load for the damaged muscles. She may be able to walk. She would have to be fitted with a brace to help support her. Wouldn't that be better than using a wheelchair her whole life?" As Mr. Hampton noticed the credulous expression on my face he added, "I know it's not a miracle cure, but at least it's a place to begin."

This all sounded preposterous to me. I didn't understand it nor did I want to try. As much as I loved Mr. Hampton, I wished he'd take this subject up with Doc Jamison instead. "Mr. Hampton, it all sounds wonderful," I answered not being at all truthful. "But Beth is so young and I'm sure it must be very expensive. Why, Helen can barely feed..."

"That's where we come in." Mr. Hampton's face lit up like a child's on Christmas morning. "We would like to set up a fund for Beth. When she's old enough, about six years of age, we'll pay for her therapy. Mrs. Hampton offered to take the train trip to stay with her when the time comes. Do you think Helen will be agreeable?"

He had my attention now. For a moment I forgot about all my duties and concentrated on what this would mean for Beth. "I'm astounded, Mr. Hampton. What a kind, generous thing to do. I'm sure Helen will be more than happy with your offer." My moment of compassion was over, as the merchandise I'd ordered was assembled and ready to go. "Now if you'll excuse me, I need to get back to the farm."

"Don't go yet," Mr. Hampton objected. "Mrs. Hampton would love it if you stopped for a visit. She'd be hurt if you didn't at least say hello."

I gave Mr. Hampton a wan smile and nodded my head. I grumbled in my heart the entire way there and am pretty sure I wasn't good company for Mrs. Hampton. She treated me graciously as always and did not take offense at my surly mood. As soon as I could get away, I trotted the horses all the way back. Their sides were heaving and they were snorting desperately to get their breath, when we hit a large rut in the road. It wasn't until I pulled the buckboard into the barn that I realized my package had fallen out. I was so mad I kicked a bucket near me which happened to be full of water. As I stood with my skirt and shoe soaked and my temper smoldering, I thought of Dorothy's rug story. The events of the day tumbled back at me in all their absurdity. All my frustration had not furthered my tasks one jot or tittle.

I began to giggle, which turned into an outright belly laugh, resounding around the barnyard as I leaned on Patches for support. John heard me and looked at me sideways, like a confused puppy looks at someone who's saying words he can't understand. "What's so funny, Rachel?"

"Just me, John. I'm the only funny thing happening around here." I related the events of the day but he didn't see anything amusing about it. "Seems normal way ta react ta me." He shrugged his shoulders and began to unhitch the horses.

I walked up to the house, thanking John for taking over. What a delightful day it could have been if I'd only looked for what God wanted to do in it. I realized my debt for this day wasn't over yet as I would have to look for my package tomorrow. Today was gone forever.

24

MY LIFE WITH TORY

The Fall Festival. Just the memory of it gave me the whim-whams. But here I was again, primping as I slipped on my blue dimity, a repeat of last year only in my appearance. But perhaps that had changed too, because I'm a firm believer in your insides affecting the way you look on the outside. All the fairy stories say so, and I absolutely trust the fairy stories.

We journeyed in the buckboard with Uncle Charles, John, and the Sowders family. Tory invited me to go with him, but Uncle Charles uncharacteristically insisted I come with them. I think he was giving me a chance to redeem the previous year. I wouldn't have had it any other way.

It was an overcast day as we set out but it dampened none of our spirits. We laughed and sang the entire way there. John, the storyteller, delighted us with tales of his friend Nathaniel, who fought Indians when the Colorado territory was being settled. I doubt a word of it was true, but he had the children wide-eyed with interest.

Shortly after we arrived, I ran into Fay. "What a great day, isn't it, Fay?" She frowned at me until her forehead looked like a sheet that had been badly folded and pressed her lips tightly together, causing her normally pleasant face to be full of lines. Panic struck me as I feared the worst. "What is it? Are you feeling all right?"

"Oh yes, I'm fine. I shouldn't pout so, but I spent hours yesterday making a custard pie and a chocolate one for today."

"Uh oh, what happened?"

"I was in a hurry as I packed them; Arthur helped me and between the two of us, we put the chocolate pie on top of the custard pie. Don't ask me how it happened." Fay led me over to the table, and sure enough, one pie was upside down on the other, only crust and goo seeping out the sides. Amazingly enough, it kept its shape so although it was upset it remained perfectly poised.

Fay's forehead was scrunching up again so I commented, "Now don't get riled, Fay. You may start a new rage in pies. All the best recipes come from accidents. Besides, 'no use crying over spilt milk'. You raised me on that adage." I winked, which caused her to break into a reluctant smile, looking for all the world like the cat that swallowed the canary.

Tory soon caught up with me and we spent the afternoon with the children. Beth was full of glee since she received so much attention in her buggy chair. Every child there wanted to push her around the park. I wished it would always be so joyful for her.

Henry loved the games and was quite proficient at them. Howard brought his stuffed rat which he and Henry planted in just the right places to scare the ladies. I had a vague feeling I should stop them, but when I saw Maggie Phlox jump, I got the giggles and enjoyed it as much as they did. Tory scolded me and I tried to feel guilty, but it just didn't work.

When it came time for dinner, we gorged ourselves like a swarm of locusts cleaning a field. Fried chicken, roast beef, pork chops, German potato salad, tomatoes and chives, coleslaw, fresh bread and preserves, and enough kinds of pies to feed the hungry. I determined to take a big piece of Fay's pie so she wouldn't feel bad that there was some left over, but when I got there, it was all gone. It was the hit of the festival. Every man there was asking his wife to combine her pies.

When the fiddles and brass began to play, we all sat quietly and listened. Soon couples were drifting out to the dance floor like butterflies floating from flower to flower. As Tory led me out, I caught sight of Garvin out of the corner of my eye. He was with Penelope Cane, a lovely shy girl quite a bit younger than Garvin. She clung to his arm and gazed into his eyes, reminding me of a little girl who looks at her father, believing he is the strongest man in the world. Garvin poured on his charm shamelessly, but he gave me a winning smile and I felt he was being sincere with young Penelope.

Besides dancing with Tory, I danced with Henry, although he obviously didn't have much use for such nonsense. He'd much rather plant Howard's rat in various places. Tory whirled Beth and Elma around, bringing screams of laughter from both of them. The only bleak spot in the evening was when I glanced at Helen. Uncle Charles offered to dance with her but she declined, making me feel like the child who got all the toys in her stocking at Christmas while the other one only got coal.

As the evening wore on, Tory asked me to take a stroll with him. Although it was still overcast and chilly, the moon would appear occasionally as if playing peek-a-boo. We walked along peacefully, saying little until we came to, of all things, a large weeping willow. Here Tory took both of my hands in his, searching my eyes as if he'd lost something in them. Words didn't come easily for Tory. From Garvin they gushed, like a pump that had been primed ahead of time. With Tory they were like a gentle rain that trickled out of a cloud on a misty day. Garvin's words tended to be like a big parade making its way through town with the bass drums, clearing the way and getting everyone's attention. Tory's built a tower that lasted for a lifetime. I knew I could count on his words.

"Rachel, I've come to appreciate you so. I can't imagine what my life was like before you came to Wesley. Every day when I'm working the farm, I think of you and picture you there by my side." He looked away from me now, as if needing relief from my gaze. "I know I'm not rich, but the farm will make a good living for both of us." He stopped now and seemed to struggle with what to say next. Finally he blurted out as if they were the last words left in him, "Rachel, will you marry me?"

Although I'd hoped and waited for this question, I didn't trust my ears when I actually heard it. I simply stared at him far too long. At last I leaned toward him, put my arms around his waist and buried my head in his chest. "Yes." It was barely a peep, then louder. "Yes, I would love to be your wife." Tory gently lifted my face and kissed me, making me joyous and nervous all at once.

As we lingered in each other's arms, I felt as secure as I'd felt since Papa died. The delicate branches of the willow enclosed us in a dreamy shelter, making me feel like I'd visited a different world altogether. "Do you know that everything important seems to happen to me under a willow tree?" I muttered, sounding to myself as if I'd drifted off to sleep and was just waking up from a dream.

"In that case, we'll plant one together in expectation of all the great events yet waiting to happen." I could tell I was speaking Tory's language now. He knew how to plant trees.

As we reluctantly drifted back to the dance, Tory said he'd speak to Uncle Charles soon. We discussed a winter wedding and then walked arm in arm, silence enfolding us like a warm quilt on a cold night. What a glorious silence it was, confident in Tory's love and basking in his presence.

When the evening ended and we parted company once more, Tory pressed a paper into my hand, "Read this when you are alone, Rachel. I love you." His touch and his words made my heart skip a beat.

The ride home went quickly. The children all fell asleep, which made my silence less noticeable. If I'd been alone, I would have been singing at the top of my lungs, so instead I sang in my heart, breaking out in a slight giggle every now and then.

As Uncle Charles and I climbed the stairs to his home, he tried to make casual conversation with me. He grinned as I looked at him in a dazed way. I tried to regain my composure enough to act normal, but I felt like a child who just got caught with her hand in the cookie jar. My mind was too full of weddings and flowers, cottages and children.

As I prepared for bed, I laid Tory's note on my pillow. I couldn't wait to read it, yet I was almost afraid to. It was similar to having a package you'd love to open, but then you knew once you unwrapped it, the surprise would be gone forever. Then the awful thought came to me that maybe it was a supply list or something awful like that. A child expecting a doll gets a shovel. I finally decided that I'd had enough foolishness. I turned the envelope over a couple of times then gently pried it open. Tory, my man of few words, poured poetry out to me. I wondered how many times he had written it over, or agonized over each line. I had to admit it wasn't Shakespeare, but it was all mine, written with just me in mind. I loved it.

Sweet Rachel, what expectation fills me

One with whom I can share my deepest thoughts,

Or my darkest secrets.

As you become my refuge,

I will become your fortress.

Surely God has brought us together to forge a future

Stronger than either of us could hope for alone.

A helpmate, a companion, a friend.

As you become my refuge,

I will become your fortress.

As God entwines us together with Him,

It will form a strand which cannot be easily broken.

All our hopes and dreams twine together.

As you become my refuge,

I will become your fortress.

I closed my eyes and fell asleep still clutching his poem.

25

THE PARLEY

It was just a couple of days until Tory came to talk to Uncle Charles but it seemed like weeks to me. I was bursting to tell someone but couldn't. When I finally saw his buggy coming, I was outside hanging up the wash. I ran to meet him as he drove up the lane.

"Hello, Tory!" I yelled above the clatter of the horses.

"Hello, Rachel. I missed you!" he yelled back. When the horses stopped and Tory tied them to the fence post, he looked at me awkwardly, as if he'd just met me in his grandmother's parlor and wasn't sure what to do with me. I knew it was up to me to break the ice.

"I loved the poem, Tory. I've read it probably twenty times since you gave it to me. It will always be one of my most treasured possessions." His face turned a bright red, but he seemed pleased.

"Is this a good day to see your uncle?"

"I think it will be fine. He'll be coming in for dinner in a few minutes. You'll join us, won't you?"

"Might as well get used to your cooking," he said with a wink, but I groaned to myself as the reality of what he said sunk in. I hoped he'd still want to marry me after dinner. But as it turned out, the meal was pretty decent. I'd been working harder at it since Tory's proposal, truly motivated to get it right. Plus, we had so much food this fall, with the garden putting out its best, that I could hardly go wrong.

Dinner was a little awkward, nonetheless, with Tory and me grinning at each other like lovesick raccoons. He tried to concentrate on talking to Uncle Charles and John while I jumped up from the table a lot to make sure everything was perfect, and to try to exorcize the monkey that was jumping up and down inside of me.

When dinner finally ended, Tory drew Uncle Charles into the sitting room as I cleared the dishes. I saw Uncle Charles turn to grin at me and nod his head as they left. I frowned to show my disapproval, but that only caused him to grin more. Tory looked nervous. I felt awful for him. I was glad the man had to ask for the woman's hand and not the other way around. The thought of my going to his mother to ask his hand in marriage gave me the heebie-jeebies something awful. I was also a little afraid of what Uncle Charles might do to Tory. The two of us had a similar sense of humor. The trouble with playing jokes on others is you're never sure when you're going to get it back.

Later I asked Tory what happened, and this is his account:

As they made themselves comfortable in the sitting room, sipping their after dinner coffee, Tory attempted some small talk which Uncle Charles was content to continue as long as possible. Finally Tory approached the subject of our marriage. "Sir, there is something of more grave importance I want to speak to you about."

"Your family isn't in any trouble are they?" Uncle Charles scrunched his face up like an orangutan. I've never seen an orangutan, but those were Tory's exact words, so I'll have to find a picture of one.

"Oh no, nothing like that. It's just that..."

"You need some help with your farm," Uncle Charles added before Tory could finish, looking now like a magpie about to peck at you. I never knew Tory could be so descriptive until he told me this story.

"Not at all. Actually the farm is doing very well. My Poland-China hogs are a profitable business. In fact, that's partly why I feel I can tell you..."

"Now I'm not interested in any business ventures. My cattle keep me busy enough." He now shook his head like a school marm scolding a student for the wrong answer. That's what Tory said. I'm not making this up.

Tory was now getting frustrated. "Mr. Bradbury, it has nothing to do with business."

"You just said that is what you wanted to tell me," Uncle Charles contradicted.

"Mr. Bradbury, I want to marry Rachel!" Tory blurted out as quickly as possible. I even heard him in the kitchen which made me jump like Jehoshaphat. I couldn't imagine why he was yelling.

Uncle Charles burst into laughter before an astonished Tory. "Why didn't you say so in the first place, man?" and he stood up and clasped his hand, eyes shining like a wolf about to shake the little rabbit to pieces. Personally, I think Tory hunts too much and has too many animal metaphors, but it did give a lively account of the experience. Of course, Tory saw the joke was on him and joined Uncle Charles in the hilarity. And I could tell by the way he told me about the encounter that he was none worse for the wear.

Before coming to me in the kitchen with their congratulations, Uncle Charles struck a serious note. "I think it will be a wonderful union, Tory. I couldn't have picked better for her myself. Take care of her for me. I'll miss her terribly."

When Tory told me that part, I cried.

Tory stayed for another hour. We planned a February wedding and talked of our future. Tory's father offered to remodel the creamery, which he owned but no longer used in town, as our first home. I wanted to see it right away, but Tory wouldn't let me. He wanted to work on it first. I reluctantly agreed but felt certain he'd change his mind before the wedding.

After he left, I danced around the house like a ballerina on the stage. It was no use trying to get anything else done today. After taking the clothes off the line, I decided to ride into town to tell Fay, and anyone else I saw, the good news. By the time I drove back to the farm, five people knew I was getting married. I even told Garvin at the bank. He congratulated me generously and I could see he meant it.

It didn't seem right to return home before telling the Sowders family, so I drove there on impulse. Helen greeted me with joy, sharing my news graciously and offering to help me get ready for the wedding. Henry took the news in stride, although he didn't react much. Wondering what was on his mind, I singled him out. "What do you think of Tory and me getting married?"

"It's fine," he answered, as if being drilled for a test.

"Maybe you could do something special at the wedding."

"Won't be no time for us no more," Henry said with a scowl.

"What do you mean?"

"You'll have kids of your own now. Can't be bothered by us." He then pulled himself up to his full three feet eight inches. "We'll be all right. Always did haf ta do for ourselves. We'll do so again."

"Henry," I lowered my voice and sat down next to him. "I'll always have time for you." I then squeezed his hand. "Tory loves you as much as I do."

I could see that he was not completely reassured, looking like a child who wanted to join in and play with the others, but not sure if he'd be accepted. His words rang in my head the next few days like a chain of bells on the sleigh. I hadn't thought about how having my own children would change things. Henry was right. It would be different now. I wouldn't be able to take the afternoon off as I'd done today to do as I pleased. It would be a difficult change, but the only one that made sense. I came to terms then with the sacrifices I'd have to make to be married. As much as I tried to think about this whole thing sensibly, my mind scattered to the wind every time I pictured Tory's face.

26

MR. PUFF'S FARM

As the days grew busier, I longed once more for some carefree time. Fay would have told me "no rest for the weary" or "man's work is from sun to sun but a woman's work is never done." However, when Tory noticed my weariness he declared authoritatively that it was time for a trip to Mr. Puff's farm.

"Who in the world is Mr. Puff?" I asked as I conjured up pictures in my mind of a jolly, rotund elf.

"Ah, we can't be married before you have been properly introduced to Mr. Puff," Tory teased with a cock of his head and a sly smile on his face. He then straightened his back, clicked his heels together, and arched his eyebrows in a dignified manner, "Mr. Puff has a farm next to my brother Edward's fine estate." Relaxing his posture with the smirk back on his face he added, "Actually Eddie hasn't built on his land yet so Mr. Puff has the only house around there. He's been a great friend of the family. We went to see him all the time as youngsters. It's a storybook type of farm; the kind in all the best tales. I always feel as though I've been away from everything when I go there."

"Oh, do let's go!" I jumped up feeling like someone had given me a tonic that fortified my blood or something like that. "I could really use an outing."

Tory smiled with sheer pleasure that I was so willing to adopt his boyhood frivolities. The next day he arrived shortly after dawn as we began the long buggy ride to Delray which was twenty miles away. Even with having to arise at an early hour, I had new energy at the thought of doing something different. The weather was crisp but sunny so we huddled together, laughing as Tory shared memories of our destination. We brought along several bushel baskets to fill with black walnuts from the woods surrounding Mr. Puff's farm.

I'm constantly amazed as I travel though Illinois how a terrain can be so flat. I searched the landscape constantly for a hill or rock but only saw an occasional clump of trees break the monotony. The few farmhouses appeared as islands between the fields of crops and sea of prairie grass. Yet, all this openness gave me a sense of freedom. I felt like running across it until I collapsed. The thrill of discovering this vastness for the first time filled me with excitement. I imagined I was the first settler to ever see this land then felt silly for my childishness.

The time passed quickly as Tory and I chatted and my mind wandered. The ride to Mr. Puff's farm was relaxing enough before I even set foot on his property, but as soon as I caught a glimpse of the place, my soul let out a satisfied sigh. The house was a little white bungalow with a green roof and shutters. There were gingerbread cutouts lining the roof and porch, making it look the way I always pictured the candy house in *Hansel and Gretel*. A porch swing painted bright red swung softly in the breeze. A dog with only three legs trotted out to greet us, acting as though we were the best thing that ever happened to him. Evidently the Puffs laundered all their linens today, because bright quilts of all colors floated up and down on the line like flags leading a procession. The barns were worn so that the red stain on them had mellowed to an auburn shade. Prairie grass framed the largest one, making it look like a giant guarded by little tin soldiers. An orchard was so full of apples that the trees looked more red than green. The black walnut woods in the distance made a backdrop that framed the perfect picture. Everywhere I looked my eyes feasted with pleasure.

Before introducing me to the Puffs, Tory took me to all his favorite spots. We filled our baskets quickly with an abundance of nuts and I tasted my first pawpaw. It looked like a small, fat cucumber and was filled with a mushy white fruit. It had been a long time since I'd tried a new food. I felt like a child who tastes ice cream for the first time. Even my appetite picked up as I gobbled up one fruit after the other.

Our favorite spot was the fresh spring running through the Delray woods. Tory showed me that upstream it was much clearer than downstream. We sat on the bank for a long while, throwing sticks in the water and watching them meander down to settle into the muddy part of the creek.

Finally, we pulled ourselves away from the mesmerizing rivulet and made our way to the farmhouse in the distance. As we neared the house, we were greeted by a great number of English sheepdog puppies, evidently the offspring of the three legged dog. She must have called the whole clan out to greet us. There were all sizes and hues and they sniffed, pawed, and yapped at us. It was an exuberant greeting that had us both giggling like school kids.

The farmhouse door swung open as a large, buxom woman came out, calling the dog's names. She stopped and squinted as she saw Tory and me, shading her eyes against the bright sun. Her hand went down and her arms shot out as recognition flooded her countenance. "Tory Hampton, I do declare! I wondered when the urge to come here would overtake you. How dare you stay away so long?" She continued chattering and scolding as she grabbed Tory in a big bear hug. After squeezing him until he was blue, she turned to me. "Now who is this pretty little thing? I bet she's the reason you've stayed away so long," Mrs. Puff winked in an exaggerated way.

"This is Rachel Scott, Mrs. Puff. She has indeed captured my attention. That's why I brought her here. She needs the fine influence of the Puff family." Tory laughed heartily as she drowned me in an embrace.

"Well, come on in and tell me all about yourselves. Mr. Puff will be in for dinner soon. I've got a big batch of meat and potatoes ready." Turning quietly to Tory, I heard her whisper, "I'll do my best to fatten her up for you." I soon found out that she took her mission seriously. "Will you go out to the milk tank for me, Tory? Bring a lot for all of us."

"I'd be delighted to, Mrs. Puff. Wait until you see what I bring back from the milk tank, Rachel," Tory said with boyish glee. I couldn't imagine what he meant. What could be so exciting about milk?

Mrs. Puff put me to work adding dishes to the table as she stirred and tasted her many pots simmering on the stove. While we were making small talk, a funny looking man came in with the longest handlebar mustache I'd ever seen. It was perfectly groomed and curled into a complete loop. I knew at once this was Mr. Puff, even more storybook than I could have imagined. He came in noisily and gave Mrs. Puff a loud kiss on the cheek, his arms unable to get around her. Yet, he seemed as pleased to see her as if she were the first lady.

Before she had a chance to introduce me, Tory came back in with a huge jug full of root beer. It seemed perfect that these people would keep root beer in the milk house instead of milk. Soon we were all sipping and laughing as

Tory told them of our engagement. They were as delighted as if Tory and I were their own children. I was enjoying the root beer so much I found it hard to concentrate on the conversation. I'd tasted root beer before, but had never had it so cold. The cold stream water running through the milk house made it icy as spring water.

Next came dinner. I couldn't believe all the food that was laid before us. I was still full of pawpaws and root beer. However, Mrs. Puff filled our plates amply with mutton, potatoes, biscuits, corn, green beans, and canned peaches. For dessert she offered us two kinds of pie. I can truthfully say I've never eaten so much or enjoyed it more.

Both Mr. and Mrs. Puff spoke constantly, almost at the same time, but were so good natured about it that it didn't seem overwhelming or rude. They were witty too, playing off each other like a comedy team. It was the liveliest meal I'd experienced. I felt I'd known them all my life and relaxed more than I had for weeks. I was already thinking of excuses to come back.

After dinner the Puffs offered to help us shell our nuts. Many were green and needed to dry yet, but those that had a ripe, black hull, we set to work on. Mr. Puff bored a hole the size of a walnut into a four by six inch board. We took a hammer and pounded the nuts through the hole, ridding them of their hulls. It was hard work but pleasant company. When we were finished, our hands were stained completely black which no amount of washing could remove. They remained that way for a full week before the last of the stain wore off.

Sadly, we decided to leave so we could make it home before dark. Before departing, Mrs. Puff showed us how her excellently trained sheep dog could round up the cattle a quarter of a mile away and bring them home in spite of her missing leg. She then offered us a young puppy as a wedding gift. As I picked up the one that squirmed the most, I thought of Ralph and Spot, my childhood friends. This pup would truly make it seem as if Tory and I were starting our own home. My own home; what a perfect thought. I hoped it would be as warm and loving as Puff's home was to us.

27

CHRISTMAS

November and December flew by the way a gust of wind scatters a pile of leaves. I wondered after we set our wedding date why we wanted a winter wedding. With getting ready for Christmas, my fingers already ached from sewing.

Christmas unfolded its timeless message, wrapping me in its festivity the way Mary swaddled her newborn babe. The moment we began singing Christmas hymns at church, I was as ready for the holiday as if it were the very first time I was celebrating it. I decided at that point to put off making my wedding dress until after the twenty-fifth. I didn't want it to overshadow the coming of the King of kings into the world. I embroidered several ornaments for the Christmas tree at church. One showed the Christ child with Mary and Joseph, another the Bethlehem star, and the last an angel proclaiming the good news, although Uncle Charles made fun of the latter, saying no self-respecting angel could possibly look the way I portrayed him. Those who could contributed by bringing an adornment from home and hanging it on the tree. In spite of Uncle Charles comments, I felt I was offering them to Christ himself as the wise men had so many years ago, even if it was not historically accurate in its portrayal.

I also made numerous gifts. Uncle Charles invited the Sowders family for Christmas dinner. I was thankful that Fay offered to fix the dinner this year so that I wouldn't have to worry about that. I crocheted mittens and scarves for each child, with a baseball design woven into Henry's. It took me a while to get the ball looking round, but it worked out nicely. For Helen, I crocheted a soft rose sweater, which I knew would bring out the color in her complexion. I made a scarf for Arthur and John and an embroidered table cloth for Fay. I worked on it for six months, off and on. I knew she would love it. Uncle Charles was the hardest to decide upon. He lived so simply that he rarely needed anything. I settled on a new Sunday shirt. Tory was the only one I purchased a gift for. From my savings, I bought him a pair of fine pearl cuff links.

I always have trouble waiting to give the gifts I make, especially when I saw how desperately the Sowders family needed their items. This year I didn't have much time to wait because I put my final touches on everything on the twenty-third. On the twenty-fourth, I spent the day with Tory and his family. It was their habit to celebrate on Christmas Eve, which worked out perfectly.

Mr. and Mrs. Hampton let us know repeatedly how delighted they were with Tory's and my engagement.

Having two grown sons, they were pleased to have a female in the family. Mr. Hampton read the Christmas story and then led us all in prayer, each of us taking a turn when he finished. After that Tory played his mandolin as we sang *Silent Night* and *God Rest Ye Merry, Gentlemen*.

Mrs. Hampton prepared a marvelous dinner with ham, of course, which was Tory's contribution to our Christmas feast, and we had ice cream which we took turns churning earlier in the day. There were also candies and cookies of every variety to nibble on throughout the day, which Mrs. Hampton had worked on for weeks.

When we'd eaten beyond the point of anything reasonable, it was gift-giving time. Tory was delighted with his cuff links. We must have thought alike because he had a dainty opal ring for me. I've never taken it off since, except to clean it. I embroidered handkerchiefs for the rest of his family, being certain that even those who are well to do always need more handkerchiefs.

The church was just across the street so we walked through the light snow for the Christmas Eve service. When it was over, we all gathered around the huge tree at the front of the church. Many people placed special gifts to family members under the tree. As names were being called out and people went forward to receive their gifts, I was startled to hear my name. I found a fancy harness with an enormous bow wrapped around it. As I ran my fingers over the beautiful workmanship, I looked up in bewilderment. Tory put his arm around me and whispered for me to read the note attached. It read:

To Rachel, our future daughter. We will give you the team of horses to go with this harness at your wedding. The purpose, of course, is that you will use them to visit us often.

Merry Christmas,

Thomas and Clara Hampton

Even though we were in church, I let out a yelp and threw my arms around them both. I'd never been given such a gift. Tory stood grinning at seeing all his favorite people in an embrace.

The following day was a whole new celebration. I could hardly believe I was going to eat another gigantic meal, but I did, even down to Fay's mincemeat pie. The Sowders family added noisy excitement the moment they walked in the door. Helen confided that this was the first time she'd celebrated Christmas properly since her parent's had died. I shuddered at the thought of what this day must be like with Lars around. My admiration for Helen grew once more as I realized all she's had to put up with, and how little she's complained about it.

Children certainly make Christmas more exciting. They lit up like fireflies when Tory brought candy canes for each of them. Uncle Charles had purchased socks and nightshirts for each of them. John made them a fine set of blocks to play with, which the younger children immediately proceeded to use to build a castle. Henry, however, sat and watched them with a satisfied air, as if he were observing children much younger than he. Soon he glanced over at his mother. Helen nodded and he left the room. When he came back, he had a large grain sack. From it he removed three large bouquets; dried arrangements of leaves, wildflowers, and decorative weeds. Each one was different and had been arranged inside a dried gourd. They were beautiful. Henry gave one to Uncle Charles and me, one to Fay and Arthur, and the third to John while Helen apologized, "I know they not be much, but wanted to do somethin'. Henry gathered them and I arranged them."

It was Fay who spoke first. "I think they are the prettiest arrangement I've ever seen. You both have quite a talent. Ours will go on the dining room hutch. Thank you for being so thoughtful." We all then chimed in with our "oohs" and "aahs".

Fay sent the Sowders family home with baskets full of food when the day was over. Before Fay and Arthur left, she pulled me aside. "Think of that woman taking time to dry flowers for us with all she has to do, and did you see how it brought that boy delight to give them to us? I hope my children will be so giving."

"I'm sure they will with you and Arthur as a model."

"You know, I think this baby is going to be all right, Rachel. It has increased my faith in God and love for others just by carrying it. I pray every night that we won't see any tragedy this year."

"I pray the same, Fay. I'm sure God means for you to be a mother. After all, He let you practice on me. He'll take care of you and your little one." I hugged her as best I could for she was getting round.

My heart was full as I walked Tory to the door. "This is the best Christmas I've ever had. I want to wrap this warm feeling of the last few days and carry it with me through the long, cold winter."

"I guess that's what Christmas is for, in a way. Even if the feelings go, we have the memory and remember how good God is to us."

I leaned into him as he gently pressed my head to his chest. The clock ticked in the corner, no other sound after this wonderful, noisy day.

28

FAY'S BABY

The New Year came in with a vengeance. The first week of January brought an ice storm that covered every tree, shrub, and blade of grass with a coating so thick it looked like everything had been encased in glass. Young trees bowed to the ground as they struggled to keep their burden from crushing them. Huge branches on large, sturdy trees snapped in two as if they were matchsticks. Uncle Charles slipped and painfully bruised his tail bone as he attempted to check on the animals. John didn't join us for breakfast for three days as the storm raged. No one left their homes for any reason.

I spent three days working on my wedding dress next to a roaring fire, feeling slightly guilty as Uncle Charles sat impatiently with a pillow on his posterior, frustrated that John had to take care of the animals without him. I offered to help, but he forbade me to step outside, except for firewood. He didn't want both of us laid up.

The day after the storm was magnificent. The sun burst through the clouds illuminating the sparkling ice as if this display was the whole reason for the tempest in the first place. Every object glistened like diamonds, so resplendent and bright that it was hard to look at it for very long. The entire world was encrusted in a shiny glaze that made the oldest worn-out tree look like a lollipop waiting to be eaten by an eager ten-year-old.

As the world began to move about once more, we learned of the damage the storm had caused. The roof over the kitchen needed repaired since several shingles came loose and blew off. Uncle Charles knew they needed to be replaced as soon as possible for when the spring thaw came, we'd have running water in our kitchen, and not the kind you want. We also lost several animals to the ice, which we butchered for meat. John dented Uncle Charles best axe trying to separate a frozen joint. Our best oak lost its largest branch, which made it look like a lopsided old man trying not to lose his balance.

Others fared far worse. The Dugan family lost their barn through the weight of the ice. Their horses and other livestock were injured or killed in the collapse. The Sowders' roof was badly damaged. Not in good shape before the storm, it now needed to be completely re-shingled. John and Uncle Charles patched it as best they could to keep the cold out, but knew that come spring, the rains would find every hole that hid from their sight at the moment.

The Hampton's home was unscathed, although Mister Hampton had some repairs to do on the store. Most of the damage in town was caused by trees snapping in two.

The Schmidt family had a tree smash right through the front of their house. The neighbors all gathered to help them repair the damage.

For months we were to hear of the mischief the ice caused. Some didn't know of the damage until it started to melt. I wondered if the wildlife could have survived such a blizzard. My mind rested about that the day after the sun came out. We had several barn cats, my favorite a gray shorthair named Smokey. After the storm, all the cats were accounted for except this feisty one. I wouldn't have been surprised if he'd been caught in the storm while pursuing a mouse. I worried about him all day and called for him until I was hoarse. At the setting of the sun, I assumed Smokey was lost forever and I railed against a world where death reigns.

In the morning I woke early to help with the chores. As I stepped onto the porch for firewood, a grey ball hurled itself at my feet. Usually too independent to sit still for anything, Smokey clung to me like a frightened child. Our normal play was for me to tickle his stomach while he pretended to bite and kick me like a tiger about to rip apart his prey. But today he was a much different cat. He curled up in my arm and began to shake all over. His eyes looked wild and unfocused. I took him inside and petted him by the fire. After feeding him some warm milk, he stopped shaking and began to purr, sounding like a quieter version of the motor on the bike that Garvin had. He had frostbite on one of his hind paws and he limped and held it high, afraid to put much weight on it. One of his ears permanently flopped over, never to straighten again. We let Smokey stay in the house after that. He and Uncle Charles recuperated together over the course of the next week and became fast friends.

Less than a week after the storm, a young boy rode out on horseback to the farm. I saw him approaching, curious as to whom it could be. I went to the door before he had a chance to knock. Up close he looked to be about ten years old, just starting to move out of boyhood into manhood. He looked up at me and swept a stray lock of hair out of his eyes in order to study me more clearly. "Are you Rachel Scott?"

"Yes, I am."

"Your sister sent me. She's my neighbor." He paused and grinned, showing a row of crooked teeth. "It's her time. Doc is there and my mom, but she wants you. Can ya come?"

I stared at him for a moment. I never have been good at emergencies. For some reason, I couldn't think of what he meant. "Time?" I murmured as my mental fog sorted out his words. "Oh! Of course, the baby. Is she all right?"

He shrugged his shoulders. "Guess so. I don't know much about these things." The lock of hair was back over his eyes, which seemed to suit him now as he blushed at the notion of birthing babies. I reached out to pat his arm. "I don't know much either, but I guess we're going to learn something today."

"You might, ma'am, but I intend to stay busy doing other things today!" The look on his face made me giggle. "Wait a minute. I'll give you a reward for your trouble." I fished through my purse and pulled out a coin, adding a leftover peppermint I found in there. He displayed his crooked teeth in all their glory as he popped it in his mouth and stuffed the coin in his pocket.

As soon as he mounted to ride out, I hurried to tell Uncle Charles. He wanted to go too, but his tail bone was much too sore for a sleigh ride. Fortunately, the day was clear as I set out on my own. It was afternoon now, so I knew I wouldn't be back until at least the morrow. I had no idea how long it took to have a baby, but I was pretty sure it wouldn't cooperate and come by supper. My prayers lifted to God like a flock of starlings lifting off the tree, one after another, swooping the tail of the one before. I was scared.

A pale, worn Arthur greeted me as I stepped into their home. "Is she doing well, Arthur?"

He furrowed his brow and turned away from me to stare out the window. My heart skipped a beat. He finally spoke, each word sounding like an anvil struck by a mallet. "I don't know, Rachel. I've never been more frightened in my life. If I lost Fay now, I don't know how I could go on." He clenched his fist so tightly that his knuckles turned white.

"Well, what's happening? Is she in danger?" I felt like slapping him to goad him to some kind of action instead of moaning like a lost child.

It worked. His head snapped up and fire flared in his eyes. "No one tells me anything! They won't let me in to see her. I've been listening to her scream. She even swore. Fay never swears!"

I had to admit that this was alarming news. I'd only heard Fay swear once when she burned an entire dinner. She'd washed my mouth out with soap more than once when she thought I said inappropriate things. My anger dissipated and I put an arm around Arthur. "I'll go see what's happening." He nodded and lowered his heard, looking again like a boy who just lost a fist fight.

As I knocked on the bedroom door, I heard Fay's groans and understood how they affected Arthur. A woman I didn't know answered the door. "You must be Rachel. Did my Louis come get you?" She gave a smile that displayed the same crooked teeth as her son.

"Yes. He did a good job. How is she?"

"She's been asking for you." She nodded her head toward the bed where Fay lay covered in sweat and looking exhausted. I went to her quickly, lifting her hand to my face. She muttered, "Hello, Rachel," and gave my hand a soft squeeze. I realized then that I'd never seen Fay looking weak before. I couldn't even remember a time when she'd been sick. She was always a tower of strength. Tears sprang to my eyes as I begged God to have mercy on her.

Doc Jamison pulled me aside, causing me to lose my grip on Fay's hand which made me feel as though I were letting her fall off the cliff. "Have you ever seen a birth before?" he asked.

"No, never. Is everything going as it should?"

He smiled, which made me feel like the sun had just come out after a week of storms. "Everything's fine. It's been a long labor, but she's very close to having the baby. She wanted you here, so I agreed."

I rubbed the tears off my face and turned back to Fay with new energy. We could face anything together as long as I knew it was going to be all right. I grabbed her hand again and held tightly, willing strength into her weary bones. Between pains she whispered to me, "I remember so well the day you were born, Rachel. It was a nice warm day and when Mother called me in to see my baby sister, I was so happy. I had to see your hands and feet and I asked Mother if you were mine. She said, 'Yes, Fay, she's yours.' She never realized how true those words were, or how much comfort and pleasure you've brought to my life."

The tears now sprang anew and my throat felt like I'd swallowed a pint of vinegar. I wanted to offer words of affection back to her, but it was impossible. Just as my composure started to return, another wave of pain rolled over her. When it subsided, she added, "I know you'll do the same for my baby if need be."

This was awful! Nothing about it seemed normal. I didn't see how she or the baby could live through all the agony. I kept glancing at the others in the room, but they seemed perfectly at ease, which was the only thing that kept me from throwing myself over Fay and wailing.

Finally, the pain intensified and when I thought she couldn't stand anymore, and that I would physically pummel the doctor, he cried, "There's the head." As I saw the brown fuzz on the round little scalp, my heart jumped into my throat. All of a sudden, all the suffering seemed worth it, even though I felt quite faint. Doc yelled orders at us, but I was too woozy, so I sat down abruptly as Louis' mom obeyed him. Before I knew it, he proclaimed that a new baby girl was in the world. I stared in complete awe at the wrinkled, red, bundle who was now yelling with all her might. Never drawn to infants before, there was nothing more I wanted than to get my hands on that baby. I knew something had changed in me forever.

Then it hit me like lightning that I'd left poor Arthur in ignorance. I flew down the stairs, yelling his name. "It's a girl, Arthur!" I threw my arms around his neck. "Little

Emily, to be exact." Arthur shook as if he'd just come in out of the cold, and in a way, maybe he had.

29

THE NIGHTMARE

January continued to be bitterly cold. It snowed a few more times, but most difficult were the raw winds and extremely low temperatures. I wasn't able to see baby Emily nearly enough due to the hazardous weather, but the times I did were like a spring thaw in my heart. Every time I looked at her I thought of Papa and how much he would enjoy her. She was such a fragile, helpless thing as all newborns are. I was awestruck each time I held her in my arms that God would entrust us with such a gift.

Tory braved the severe weather in order to see me. My wedding dress wasn't finished, although I worked on it at every opportunity. However, the tatting of the lace around the high collar and fitted sleeves were done and the soft folds of the satin flowed over me as I worked on it, reminding me of a waterfall I'd seen once in a photograph. I prayed for our marriage with each stitch I made, surprised by beauty inside and out.

Because of the cold, I worried each time Tory set out for home. Even inside the house, the temperature was icy. I never wanted to leave the stove. I'm sure I did more baking during January than ever before or since. We even slept downstairs several nights because it was just too cold upstairs.

Early one morning after Uncle Charles and John returned from their chores, there was a rap on the door. As I opened it quickly to pull whoever it was in before much heat escaped, I was startled to see Sheriff Miller. He nodded to me like he was dismissing me from duty and asked to speak to Uncle Charles. I showed him to the sitting room and waited anxiously as they spoke in muffled tones. It made me feel like a child who's been banished from the room so the grown-ups can talk. At last Uncle Charles called for me to come in.

"Rachel," he said looking like Job himself, "Lars has escaped. He jumped the guard yesterday and fled. We've no idea where he is or if he could survive this cold. The sheriff is forming a posse to look for him. I'll go along and John can come too. Will you go get Helen and the children? It's likely he may go there, although he hadn't a few hours ago when the sheriff checked. We'll occupy the house with some men as soon as the family is safely here." Uncle Charles bent over as if he were in physical pain. "Poor Helen." He shook his head as he clutched his stomach. "What more does that woman have to bear?"

I said nothing; only nodded in response. I'm ashamed to say that my first response was dread at having to go out in the cold for any reason, but I knew the men needed to finish gathering a posse. I gathered blankets to cover the children and put on several extra layers over my own clothes. When I finally felt I had enough on to face the frigid cold, I stepped out onto the porch. The blast of cold that hit my face caused it to hurt, so I wrapped my scarf around every inch of skin, until only my eyes were showing. They were so cold that I blinked just to give them relief.

I harnessed Lady, knowing I'd need her feistiness to get there and back as quickly as possible. My fingers hurt through my mittens, even though I kept them moving the whole time. I went back in the house for an extra pair of gloves to put underneath my bulky wool mittens and for the brick I'd heated to put at my feet so they wouldn't become frostbitten.

Lady could hardly wait. The horses hadn't been out much because none of us went anywhere in this weather. She snorted and her nostrils turned white from the warm air that escaped and froze on her muzzle. But I have to hand it to her; she took off at a trot and kept it up the whole time. I actually tried to slow her down to reduce the breeze because I was so cold.

Arriving at the Sowders' home, I jumped down as quickly as possible and made my way to the front door, carrying all the blankets with me to warm them before starting out again. I paused at the stoop, surprised at how quiet it was. Usually the sound of children drifted outside, but not a cough or laugh came to me now. I knocked softly at first, then harder when no one answered. Finally the door handle clanked and opened to a wide-eyed Howard looking out at me. Usually he greeted me with joy but today he grabbed my skirt and sobbed. My heart skipped a beat and I stepped into the dark house, trying to adjust my eyes after the brilliance of the snow outside. It felt like I'd entered a cave.

I finally noticed that there were no lamps lit and that the fire in the hearth was almost out. Only a few embers glowed beneath the ashes. Howard still clung to my skirts and I noticed two more small figures sitting by the fire. Then I saw Helen. She had her back turned to me as she slumped over the table, her head down on her arms. I rushed over to her but when I touched her shoulder, she screamed and lifted her head to look at me, as if I'd just appeared from nowhere. Her eyes locked onto me but didn't focus. I felt invisible.

But worse, still, was her face. I'd never seen anyone's face look like that. One of her eyes was swollen completely shut and a tear in her cheek trickled blood down her chin and onto her dress, which was torn and dirty, her bodice exposed from the rip. Her top lip had grown twice its normal size and a tooth was sticking straight out of her mouth. There were bruises on her neck and her hair hung in strings around her face, as if trying to hide this desolation from sight.

I stared for too long, but finally croaked out, "Oh, Helen, what happened?" I said it so quietly I wasn't sure whether I'd actually said it out loud or just thought it. I still don't know, because Helen didn't say a word. I tried to wrap my arms around her but she startled like a deer who just found out you were standing there.

Feeling helpless, I said the next logical thing. "Helen, come on, let's gather the children and go to Uncle Charles'. It's dreadfully cold in here." Helen still sat silently as if turned to stone by an evil magician, her head once more down on her arms. I glanced around the room, looking for anything warm to wrap the children in. I thought of Henry; he'd help me. "Henry, where are you? I need you." There was no answer and I looked nervously about, hoping against hope that he was just being stubborn. Howard, who was still clinging to me as if he was about to fall off a cliff, answered, "He's gone. Pa took 'im."

My knees buckled and I hit the bed that I'd been stripping for its blankets. Howard tumbled on top of me and hot tears flowed from my eyes, leaving warm streaks on my cold skin. I grabbed Howard and hugged him, fighting the urge to sob. I clung to him and rocked back and forth, willing myself to get past this and do the next thing. Daniel in his lion's den could not have felt more surrounded than I felt at that moment. I was almost too numb to pray, throwing the whole thing up to God to sort out until I could think clearly.

I slowly stood up, setting Howard aside and gathering every blanket in the place. I asked him to throw another log on the fire, as I wrapped blankets around his brother and sister who were shivering with chattering teeth, almost unable to move. I crossed over to the other side of the room to pull the quilts off the other bed, when I heard a whimper. It almost sounded inhuman, and it took me a moment to realize it came from Beth's crib. I rushed to look in. She was lying there, barely able to cry. Her lips were blue and her complexion splotchy. I tried to pick her up, but couldn't lift her, realizing she'd frozen to her blankets. Evidently she'd urinated, and unable to move by herself, she'd frozen to her bed.

The numbness that had overtaken me ended in a scream. The children stared at me with blank expressions as I burst into tears and began pounding the wall beside me. Helen lifted her head and all my anger came out to her. "How could you do this?" I shrieked, "You are still Beth's mother and she needs you!"

The tears welled in Helen's eyes and gut wrenching sobs shook her body. It reminded me of a possum I'd found caught in a trap once - the horrible sounds of creature who is suffering beyond measure. I felt wretched for yelling at her, but maybe crying was better than feeling nothing. Fay slapped me once as a child when I was hysterical, to get me to calm down. Maybe this was similar, in reverse.

At any rate, I couldn't afford to feel guilty; I had to keep going. I picked up Beth, mattress and all, wrapping her in two quilts. I dragged Helen and the children out into the sleigh and headed for the nearest house. Fortunately, the

Freemans lived only half a mile away. I spurred Lady on so that we reached there in a few minutes. I dragged Beth in first, without even knocking, and thrust her into Mrs. Freeman's arms with orders to hold her tight by the fire. The woman looked alarmed, but did as I told her. I ordered Mr. Freeman to take Lady to the barn while I brought the rest of the family in.

When we were all assembled again, I explained the situation, and we all set to work. Mrs. Freeman heated water until it was tepid and began to bathe Beth until she began to wail loudly which we took as a good sign. As soon as Beth's normal color returned, Mrs. Freeman found another dress for Helen after I'd washed all the blood off her face, and pressed her tooth back into position. She let me tend to her as if she were a small child.

Mr. Freeman left immediately to find the sheriff and let him know that Lars had Henry. When I told him this piece of information, my voice cracked again and I felt like a boulder was resting on my lungs. Helen's face crumpled in pain that had nothing to do with her bruises.

Finally, I felt as if everyone was reasonably taken care of, so I asked Mrs. Freeman if I could lie down for a moment. I wasn't tired, but I needed to be alone. She graciously led me to one of the bedrooms, and I fell on the bed and cried as soon as she closed the door. I tried to pray but my thoughts were confused. As I lay on the bed, staring out the window, I begged God to muddle through the mess in my mind and bring some order to it. As soon as I prayed it, I felt some kind of peace. I had no idea if anything was going to work out in this terrible disaster, but I knew that God was in control. He was with Henry when I could not be. I prayed Henry would have the same peace.

I sat up on the bed as Lars' words came echoing back to me the day he broke into Uncle Charles' house. He'd threatened to kill me and that Henry would pay. Of course. He was going to our house. He probably wanted money and revenge. He may be there now, waiting. I had to tell the sheriff.

I rushed out to explain to Mrs. Freeman where I was going, ignoring her protests about the day getting late. I pulled Lady away from her hay in the barn and put her to work again as I set out for town. After making several inquiries, I found the men meeting in Mr. Hampton's store around the potbellied stove, Mr. Freeman among them. To my amazement, they listened to me and decided to head for Uncle Charles' place immediately. As they rushed out, I sat down on one of the barrels, startling when I felt an arm around me.

"I'm sorry you had to go through all that." I looked at Tory's face as he leaned down to give me a quick kiss on the cheek. I hadn't noticed he was among the group and felt myself relax in his presence. But not even he could meet my deepest needs now.

As soon as the men rose to leave, Uncle Charles approached me. "I'm sorry we sent you to the Sowders' place alone." He looked down at his boots. "I guess I'm just not used to expecting evil."

My answer surprised me even as I said it, for I'd been feeling sorry for myself. "It's all right, Uncle Charles. I'd probably feel even worse if I hadn't been there to help."

As everyone left, I lingered by the warmth of the potbellied stove. It occurred to me that I was stuck in town for the night, so I made my way to Fay's. After putting Lady in the carriage house, I went inside and remained amazingly calm as I told Fay the whole story. She made me hot chocolate and murmured reassurances as I rocked Emily for what seemed hours. The shadows grew long and Arthur read to us as Fay fed Emily and I did needlework. I wondered if I would sleep at all this night, when we heard a rap on the door. I was delighted to see Tory there.

"Your hunch was right, Rachel. Lars went to your uncle's looking for money at the least. He took what he could find and left Henry."

I clutched my hands together, afraid to ask the next question. "Is Henry all right?"

"He's fine on the outside. He sure must be hurting on the inside though."

Just the thought sent the tears again, and Tory held me as I pulled myself together. "You too, Rachel. What an awful day."

"You're telling me. I'll never set foot in the Sowders' house again. Has anyone seen Lars?"

Tory shook his head. "No sign of him. The snow's packed hard so there's no trail to follow. We're going to look for him again in the morning. Gib Poluki had a hunch he'd be hiding at the old Becker place."

Tory left almost as soon as he got to Fay's, and I finally gave up and went to bed. It was a restless night's sleep that seemed endlessly long. Every few hours I woke with a nightmare, feeling as though I'd never be safe again. I was glad when dawn broke, helping me understand all the better how Jesus is the light of the world.

As soon as the sun was up in full, I mounted Lady and headed home. Henry was there alone since Uncle Charles and John were both with the posse. He sat by the fire and barely looked at me when I walked in. I slipped down beside him and put my arm around his shoulder. He nudged me off and continued to stare into the fire. "Do you want to talk about what happened?"

"Nope."

"Okay." I stood up and looked back down at him. He was so small. "I'll fix some breakfast. Can you eat?"

He nodded.

We spent the day circling each other the way two bulls stand each other off, waiting for the other to make the first move. I felt only relief that he was safe, but he could only think of his father. At least that's what I think he was thinking of. I really don't know since he wouldn't talk to me. A couple of times, I felt like giving him a piece of my mind, but each time the words died on my lips, unable to add another iota to his suffering.

Finally, Uncle Charles came in as the sun dipped below the horizon. He glanced at Henry and nodded his head toward the kitchen so that we could talk alone. As soon as we walked into the room, he closed the door and sat down on a kitchen chair with a thud. "No sign of him. We searched all day, everywhere we could think and couldn't find him at all. It's like he's vanished into thin air. I don't know what to think."

We sat in silence, we two, at a loss to even form our next words. After a quiet evening, I collapsed into bed and fell asleep listening to Henry sob in the room next to me.

30

HELEN AND THE CHILDREN

The next day, I set out to fetch Helen and the children from the Freeman's. Henry came with me, glad to have something useful to do. The Freeman's looked relieved to be rid of the large clan that had invaded their home, but they had done their part without complaining. As soon as Helen saw Henry, she hugged him fiercely, crying "I'm sorry" over and over. Henry threw his little arms around her, comforting her as if he was the parent and she was the child. "It's all right, Mama. We're going to be okay now." I marveled at the eternal hopefulness of youth.

We had just made it inside Uncle Charles' farmhouse when he walked in, looking like death warmed over. Helen took one look at him then nodded. "He's dead, isn't he." She said it like a statement, not a question, as if this were general knowledge that only needed a conformation.

"Let's talk in the parlor, Helen. Rachel can watch the children."

"I want to come with you." Henry spoke firmly, looking at his mother, no doubt in his mind that she'd comply.

She nodded and put an arm around him, leading the way into the sitting room. I took the rest of the children into the kitchen to make them some hot chocolate as we sat by the stove. I entertained them as best I could, but my mind kept wandering to the next room. Shortly Helen came in and sat down amongst her children. It was hard to believe that this was the same person who was so helpless two days ago. Although her eye was still swollen and her face had turned the awful green and yellow of old bruises, she spoke resolutely— confidently—as if she had thought through these circumstances for days and arrived at the best course.

She gathered the little ones around her like a flower attracts bees. They hovered and plopped down on her, grateful to have their mother back. "I have to tell you the awful news that your father has died." I was amazed by her composure. The tears were gone and certainty had taken their place. "He didn't suffer. He just stopped in someone's barn for the night and because of the cold, he went to sleep and never woke up." Elma began to cry and Helen pulled her in a close embrace. "It is a sad thing when someone dies, even someone who has been mean to you. I'm sad, too, but I know that God has good plans for us and that he will not abandon us. He's promised to be a father to orphans. You will have the best possible father now." Howard began to sniffle now, too, but Henry's jaw clenched tight, refusing to let us see it tremble.

"Uncle Charles said we can stay with him until we find out what we should do next." I smiled to myself at how she'd adopted him as an uncle to all of them. "Things are going to be different now. I don't know how, but I know our life is going to be good. I don't want any of you to worry."

They all settled in by the stove and sat there for what seemed hours. Helen hummed and rocked, stroking her children's hair and faces as if seeing them for the first time. They didn't move again until I began to work on dinner, all of them chipping in to help, alive again after a long death.

Tory and I postponed our wedding for a month, because I was needed here. It also wouldn't be right to leave Uncle Charles alone in the house with Helen and the children. I just imagined what Maggie Phlox would do with that bit of information.

During the next few weeks, Helen and I became as close as sisters. She had a new hunger to know God, giving us a starting place for every conversation. I'd never talked about God so much in my life, and I found that as I shared what I knew, it strengthened my own faith. Every day Helen's bruises faded, but her faith grew. I saw a new poise and dignity transform her harried look. She often pulled her hair into a bun and worked harder at making sure she and the children were clean and presentable. Sometimes she seemed like a completely different person than the downtrodden, mousy woman I'd known before. I always thought she was pretty, but now she blossomed like a rose that opens up when given plenty of water and sunlight.

Still, there was no clear direction in her life. She had no home or way to earn her livelihood. We worried about it together and asked God to provide. The children joined in this prayer with the complete confidence that only children have that all will be well. As our expectancy grew as thin as the clothes on their backs, the children would bolster us with comments like, "I can't wait to see what God is going to do," or "I wonder what He has planned for us." Howard asked daily if God had given them a home yet, seeing it as a fact; just a matter of when, not if.

Henry became more of the little man he always was. He'd pat his mother's back daily, telling her everything would be fine. He even talked about what he would do to support her. Once in a while he became sullen and I longed to reach into his mind to see what was there, but he would not allow it.

However, one day while we were peeling potatoes, he asked, "Miss Rachel, do you think my pa coulda changed the way Mr. Pierce did?"

I hesitated before I answered, even though I'd asked myself the same question a thousand times. "I didn't know your father very well, Henry, but anyone can change if they let Jesus Christ do the transforming. In the book of Corinthians, it says we become a 'new man in Jesus Christ, the old passes away.'"

Henry looked thoughtful, then pained, as he shed the first tears I'd seen since that awful night following his abduction. He yelled through his tears, "Why didn't he let Jesus change him? Why? Why?" Helen looked over at me and I felt I was near tears myself as I hugged Henry close to me, kneeling down to his level. "I don't know, Henry," I whispered. "We can't decide for someone else. All we can do is decide for ourselves."

Henry cried a moment more, then dried his eyes and straightened his back. He never mentioned his father again.

The reason it was so hard for me to answer Henry's question, was that I had the same kind of questions for God about Sowders' suffering. Sometimes it's awful to be human, to feel all the pain of sin and to not understand a bit of it. And yet, that is what faith is all about; to know that there is One who can redeem us in the middle of our helplessness. I needed Him as never before, maybe even all the more because I knew I'd never completely understand Him.

And I could see His hand, even in the awful events of that day. If Beth had not needed immediate care, we would have gone on to Uncle Charles' home and found Lars waiting for us there. What would have happened then? I saw too His leading as he brought to mind what I needed to know that day about where Lars would be. I even saw His mercy in Lars' death; that he was able to just fall asleep and not face a gun battle or whatever else might have awaited him. It made me want to trust Him all the more, since I knew so little myself.

That was how I was able to trust that God knew what He was doing when Helen received a letter from an aunt in Chicago during the second week of February. She expressed sympathy for Helen's tragedy and offered her home to the family. At first Helen flatly refused to consider it. I didn't know whether to encourage it or not, because the thought of them all leaving filled me with sadness. Uncle Charles, on the other hand, had no qualms.

"Why wouldn't you go with her, Helen?"

Helen looked down and fussed with the dishtowel in her hand, folding and refolding it before answering. "After my parents died and I married Lars, she wrote me a hateful letter. She told me that I'd betrayed my mother's and father's memories and that I'd live to regret it all my days." Helen now held up the dishtowel to her face, rubbing it softly against her cheek. "We haven't written since then."

Uncle Charles took her hand and sat down next to her. "In light of all that's happened, she wasn't too far wrong."

Helen winced when he said this, but she didn't pull her hand away. "And it says a lot that she would offer her home to you. Did you get along with her before your marriage to Lars?"

Helen nodded, "She was my favorite aunt. I loved her. I think that's why it hurt so much when she abandoned me."

"Then it's time to forgive her and see this as an answer to prayer."

I could see that Helen was trying to take his words to heart, but she squeezed her eyes shut to stop the tears. Uncle Charles looked at me and I scooted next to Helen and hugged her to me. "Why is this so hard, Helen?"

"I don't know." Now the tears ran down her cheek without stopping. Uncle Charles felt uncomfortable. "I'll let you ladies talk this out. I've got chores to do."

As soon as he left, I felt I knew what to say. "Is it because you don't want to leave here?" I asked barely above a whisper, thankful we were alone.

She nodded and a new torrent of tears threatened as she sobbed the words out. "I'm so ashamed of myself. I think I hoped that Charles would fall in love with me. I love him so much."

Somehow I knew that was what she was going to say, although she'd never breathed a word of it to me before.

But I could tell by the way she melted in his sight that he was the world to her. "Don't be ashamed, Helen. It's natural that you would fall in love with him since he's been so good to you, but God must have something completely different in mind for your life. I know when you get your heart set on one thing that it's hard to even think about another. But it will be best if you move on. Uncle Charles and I have talked about this. It will be best for your children if you get a new start away from all the strikes against them here. You have to think of them now."

Somehow these words closed a door for her and opened another. She dried her tears and raised her shoulders, changing the tone of her voice to the confident mother she'd become. "Of course, you're right. I'll write Aunt Martha and tell her right away. She's a widow and probably needs us as much as we need her."

In less than a fortnight, we packed all their belongings and saw them to the station. I hugged Helen fiercely and kissed the children repeatedly. This family had done far more for me than I'd done for them. Through them I learned my own weaknesses and came to understand who God is and how patient He is with us. But I was weary of goodbyes. I longed for heaven where we'd never be separated from one another again.

31

MAGGIE

Four days before the wedding, I made a trip into town to check on all the arrangements. My spirit soared as the day drew near, the way a fledgling bird must feel when it first takes flight. It was a good balm for the loneliness I felt with the Sowders' departure.

As I neared town, the hustle and bustle of activity tickled my fancy like a puppy about to enter a fray. I felt that kind of nervous excitement that makes it hard to sit still. I tied Lady and Patches to the hitch and skipped into the bakery. The smell of fresh bread wrapped itself around me, making me hungry even though I'd just eaten an hour ago.

I approached the counter to give the baker some ceramic doves I wanted placed on our wedding cake. They were a gift from Emily, which she hand-painted and sent to me. I carefully unwrapped them, thinking of my sister, the wedding, and all I had to be thankful for, when a high-pitched, whining voice broke through my daydreams. My heart sank as I turned to face Maggie Phlox. In her mid-thirties, her hair was beginning to grey at the sides, and she had a double chin, although she wasn't particularly fat elsewhere. Her husband was a successful silversmith, so she dressed in the latest fashions made of the finest fabrics. To me she looked like a package full of coal promised to a naughty child at Christmas, beautifully wrapped but dark and sinister inside.

"If it isn't Miss Scott," she said sounding like a hunter who's just come across her prey.

"Hello, Mrs. Phlox."

"Are you busy getting ready for your wedding? I hope your future in-laws are helping with the expenses. It must be a terrible burden for you to bear alone, since you have no family to help you."

I breathed a quick prayer to keep from saying something I would eternally regret. "It's no burden, Mrs. Phlox, only a joy."

"Come now, how are you paying for it? With money from your little sewing business?" The way she pronounced the double "s" in business sounded like a snake.

"I'm managing quite well, thank you," and bit my tongue, knowing I'd sounded sharper than I intended. I didn't need to give her any reason to find more fault.

"Aren't we testy today"" Maggie turned her attention to the baker, ordering large quantities of bread, cake, doughnuts and cookies. I wanted to duck out while she was occupied, but I had one more thing to ask the baker. Before I could get a word out to him, she struck again. "What does Garvin Pierce think of you marrying Tory?"

She grinned like a cat who's just stuffed a mouse in his jaws. I felt my cheeks burn hot, frustrating me all the more for fear of how she would interpret that. "I believe he's happy for us," I muttered, wondering why I bothered to answer at all.

"Mmm, I just wonder..., first you go into the country alone with Garvin Pierce then you visit Lars Sowders in jail. You haven't proven yourself a very good judge of character since you've come here. I wonder that the Hamptons would have you marry into their family." The entire time Maggie spoke, she looked down, fussing with her gloves. When she finished, she threw her head back and took a noble pose, as if she'd done a great thing by making such a bold statement.

My impulse was to gather my doves into their box and leave immediately, but a better plan came to mind as I remembered a tidbit from the past. "I'm surprised to hear you say that, Mrs. Phlox," and I struggled to keep from looking smug. When I visited Lars Sowders in jail, I overheard him mention your husband's name. He seemed to think Mr. Phlox should help him. Now why do you suppose he thought that?" I cocked my head and looked at her as if I had no idea.

She clenched her fists at her side and began to shake all over, reminding me of a bird that fluffs its feathers to stay warm in the winter. Her voice sounded like the low rumble of a volcano that was about to explode. "How dare you implying my husband would be involved in a scandal!" I was afraid for a moment that she was going to hit me. I think she would have if we hadn't been in a public place.

"Don't worry, Mrs. Phlox. I will never mention a possible link between your husband and Lars Sowders to anyone else. I wouldn't have spoken of it at all, if you had not been so rude to me. I thought you should know what it feels like. You take a tiny piece of information and make all sorts of judgments upon people without knowing the whole. A tongue can sometimes cause more wounds than a knife." I said all this gently, in as quiet a voice as possible, truly wanting her to change and not just to get revenge. Maggie quit shaking and stuttered several times trying to say something. Finally she gathered her hoard of baked items and marched out of the building. I felt reasonably sure she wouldn't bother me again.

I stared at the door a moment then turned back to the baker, noticing that he was looking down with a smirk on his face. He might have said something if Sarah Mae hadn't come in. "Rachel, I can't wait until the wedding. Is everything ready?"

"I believe it is. I think it's really going to happen."

She sighed with a look of a puppy who hopes to get chosen next out of the litter. "I hope it happens to me someday."

"I'll be sure to aim for you when I throw my bouquet." Then I added hesitantly, "What about Ben? Is he still attentive?"

She smiled and nodded, "Very. Maybe the bouquet will be the thing that pushes him over the edge," and she hugged me, washing away the frustration I'd felt just a few moments before with Maggie. I still couldn't believe it was happening to me.

32

OUR UNION

The day finally came. The snow melted early in March and turned unseasonably warm. After the harsh winter, it looked as if spring gripped the landscape and shook all the bitterness out of it. Three springs I'd been in Wesley. It's amazing how three springs could change my life so completely.

The Hamptons decorated their fine home with calla lilies and vines, transforming it into a tropical garden for our wedding. We planned a morning wedding so that we wouldn't have all day to sit around getting nervous. I woke up with butterflies floating in my stomach and my eyes. I couldn't decide whether I was nervous or excited. Both, I'm sure.

The ceremony itself went so quickly that I felt I'd held my breath the whole time. After we made our pledges "to have and to hold", the tension left and I began to enjoy this wonderful day. Everyone I loved was there. The Sowders family came back looking better fed and rested than I'd ever seen them. Helen found a job as a typist at the *Chicago Sun Times*, bringing extra income to her family for the first time. She'd come to love and appreciate her aunt whose large home had been filled with love and laughter. We'd had a joyous time together as they stayed with us a few days before the wedding. Only Tory received more attention from me than Henry. I'd missed him so much that it brought tears to my eyes when he hugged me after the ceremony.

Even more surprising was Aunt Agnes' arrival from Missouri. I'd written her about it only to inform her, never dreaming she'd attend. Uncle Charles knew she was coming but kept it a secret from me. She stayed with Fay and walked into the Hampton's house on the morning of our wedding. I couldn't have asked for a better gift.

I have to admit I loved being the center of attention on this one day. Aware that this was probably the only chance in my life to feel like royalty, I refused to feel guilty. Perhaps that's why so many brides have trouble. After being treated as a queen one day, the next they must cook, clean, and mend as if nothing happened.

When Tory slipped the wedding ring on my finger, I barely registered what was happening, but I couldn't take my eyes off it afterwards. Not that it was ornate—it wasn't— but what it symbolized still amazed me. I stared at that ring all week. Whenever this seemed like a dream, I looked at my finger as tangible proof that I truly was Mrs. Hampton.

After the wedding, Tory took me to our home, the remodeled creamery. He'd kept his word; I wasn't allowed a glimpse inside until our wedding day. He, Arthur and Fay did all the work on it. Before going inside the house, Tory took me to the stable. A roan and a dapple gray stood sentry with a ribbon tied around each of their necks. The team to go with our fancy harness! I never dreamed I'd have so much so soon.

Fay decorated my home exactly as I wanted it. Although small, it was cozy and just right for the two of us. We'd eventually build on the land nearby where the Poland-China hogs were. As he promised, Tory planted a weeping willow near where our house would be in honor of my childhood memories, my faith, and my commitment to Tory, all of which took place under this graceful tree. But for now this creamery felt like home.

It consisted of a parlor, dining room, and kitchen downstairs, all sparsely furnished but serviceable. Fay picked out soft blue paint for the kitchen, French design wallpaper for the dining room, and a deep tan for the parlor. The furniture was mostly mix and match pieces from the Hamptons and Uncle Charles. Fresh flowers graced several tables and sunlight streamed through the sheer curtains on the long windows. My only contribution to the house was a quilt I made for Tory. Fay put it on the bed for me, surprising Tory on this visit.

After settling in, Tory went out to tend the horses. I wandered about our home thanking God for more blessings than I could count. I pondered my past and how it led me to this point, realizing how important the decisions are we make and how they determine what our life will be. How could Fay and I have known that a trip to Illinois would open the door to our futures? What if I hadn't listened to God's whispers to me about taking Henry under my wing? Think of the joy I would have missed.

33

THE REWARD

The years have come and gone. Tory and I now live in a large home on the farm and have two lovely children, almost grown; a boy named Thomas and a girl named Laura. Tory has been successful with his Poland-China hogs. He now has a farrowing house and a sale barn on the grounds. He has sold hogs for well over a thousand dollars each and men come from many states to his sales, Mr. Wrigley of chewing gum fame counted among them. He invited Tory to his home on Lake Geneva, Wisconsin once, which made me jealous to no end. Tory is now speaking of buying another farm.

I finally made it to Montana to see Adam and Emily. My daughter Laura accompanied me as we encountered our first peaceful Indians and met the famous western painter, Charles Russell. I couldn't help reflecting how different my life would have been if I'd settled there, but that's so much water under the bridge.

Not all has been happy in these years. Fay has three children now. However, when she was carrying her third child, Arthur fell off one of his telephone poles and died instantly from a broken neck. We've become closer as sisters and depend on one another for everything. It's my turn to take more of the leadership in our relationship.

I lost track of the Sowders family as the children began to grow into adulthood. Mr. and Mrs. Hampton did provide for Beth's therapy and although one leg is badly deformed, she can walk with the use of a brace.

Henry is often on my mind, for I love him still after all these years. He was, after all, the first child I ever loved. One ordinary day when the children were at school, I stopped peeling my potatoes when I heard a knock on the door. I rinsed my hands off, drying them on my apron as I opened the door to see a large, handsome young man with brown hair and such engaging eyes that it startled me. He had a commanding appearance as if all matters would be set right because of his presence. He looked vaguely familiar although I couldn't place where I might know him from.

"Rachel Hampton?" he asked in a voice that reminded me of a baritone singer I'd heard once in an opera.

"Yes, I'm Rachel Hampton."

"Do you remember me? I'm Henry Sowders."

"Henry! Look at you! It's been such a long time. Come in. I want to hear all about you." I pulled off my apron and offered him some tea. "How is everyone?"

"We're all well. Mother volunteers at the hospital, besides managing the office at *The Sun*. Her bosses felt that if she could keep all us kids in line, the office help would be a breeze." We both laughed. It felt great. "Howard is married with four children, one set of twins. He works on the railroad. Calvin died shortly after his tenth birthday from diphtheria. Did Mother write you that?"

"Yes. I cried for days." He looked sad for a moment, but picked up courage and moved on.

"Elma is newly married. Her husband is a country doctor. They make a wonderful team. She loves to tell Howard's children about how she used to be the proud owner of a rat muff." We both laughed out loud at that memory.

"What about Beth? I think of her so often."

"She's doing well, always unselfish, doing things for others. She's an inspiration to us all and a big help in my work.

"And you, Henry, what are you doing?"

"I've started a home for boys." Henry's eyes twinkled and I thought how much they'd changed since they narrowed in anger like his father's. "We have humble beginnings but I have dreams of bigger things. There are so many immigrants in Chicago and more orphans than you would believe. Of course, there are lots of orphanages, but most just provide food and housing. I emphasize helping the boys find an area of interest, such as sports, music or art, something that will fill their time and make them feel good about themselves. We also talk about the importance of knowing God; that He will be with them when all others have deserted them. We even act out our Bible stories of all the great heroes after supper, just as you used to do with me when I was young. We're just one house right now, but I hope to see us expand throughout the city as others feel called to this work."

As Henry spoke, I became aware that my throat hurt even though I was smiling broadly. When I couldn't fight it anymore and my eyes grew moist and red, Henry became awkward, lowering his voice. "I know, I'm doing for others what you did for me. That's why I'm here today, to thank you for everything."

I dried my tears with the handkerchief I always kept tucked in my sleeve. Before he left I promised to visit his work in the city soon. As he drove off, I watched from beneath the weeping willow. It had grown tall and sturdy into a beautiful shelter, a reflection of how God's love had grown in me.

ABOUT THE AUTHOR

JoHannah Reardon blogs at www.johannahreardon.com.
If you enjoyed this book, please give it a positive review.
Also, check out her other books:

Christian Fiction: *Cherry Cobbler, Redbud Corner, Crispens Point, Journey to Omwana, Prince Crossing*
Children's Fiction: *The Crumbling Brick*
Family Devotional: *Proverbs for Kids*